THE COLOR OF MY SOUL

ALSO BY MELANIE S. HATTER

FICTION

Taking the Shot

THE COLOR OF MY SOUL

Melanie S. Hatter

Washington Writers' Publishing House
Washington, DC

This book is a work of fiction. Names, characters, places and incidents
are products of the author's imagination, or are indeed historical
figures and events used in a fictional situation.

COVER DESIGN by Wendy Henderson
TYPESETTING by Barbara Shaw

LIBRARY OF CONGRESS CATALOGUING-IN-PUBLICATION DATA
Hatter, Melanie S.
  The color of my soul / Melanie S. Hatter.
      p. cm.
  ISBN 978-0-931846-98-4 (pbk : alk. paper)
  I. Title.
  PS3608.A8656C65 2011
  813'.6—dc23
                                    2011026501

Printed in the United States of America

WASHINGTON WRITERS' PUBLISHING HOUSE
P. O. Box 15271
Washington, D.C. 20003

ACKNOWLEDGMENTS

I am most grateful to so many people who have shepherded me to this point in my life—it would take many pages to list everyone.

Thank you to the Washington Writers' Publishing House for accepting my novel and guiding me through to publication; to Wendy Henderson for her creative vision in designing the cover; to Feiven Zigita and Karen Robin for their sharp eyes proofing and editing; to the writing program at Johns Hopkins University, in particular Margaret Meyers, Ed Perlman and Mark Farrington— their wise words and encouragement kept me writing; to Felicia Mason, whose own writing success inspired me; and to the various writing groups that have provided support and shared my angst and passion for writing.

1993

1

KIRA FRANKLIN sat on her couch drinking her fourth vodka and tonic, bewildered by a revelation about her heredity, while Alex Harper lay in bed with a woman he had met only three hours earlier trying to forget the significance of his heritage.

Kira and Alex had met the day before...

2

KIRA SLIPPED through the colorful beaded curtain from the back of Big Bear's Cabin into the shop front; her perspective shifted from history to souvenirs representing a culture struggling to find its footing. The interview had ended. John Harper, known to most as Big Bear, keeper of the family history, of his people's history, sat in the office behind her. His stories had gone back to the 1700s, stories passed through generations, stories of the great Chief Gray Wolf and his sons Quiet Hawk and Long Arrow, stories of war, of grief, of survival. Laid out before her were links to the past: Native American jewelry and trinkets in glass cases, paintings and sculptures in every nook, and mobiles hanging from every beam. Her mind was awash with images and people she wanted to write about. She would be back. This story — a story about the local Indian community reclaiming ancestral land, re-affirming their heritage — was too good, too important.

She stood in the shop regaining her sense of the present. A young man, a third generation of Harpers, leaned over a glass jewelry case. She had spied his long slim legs upon her arrival. As she approached him, a spicy fragrance greeted her. He carefully placed on the black velvet a silver wolf pendant, designed so that strands of silver imitated the animal's fur, its eyes two turquoise gems.

"That's beautiful," Kira said so quietly she wasn't sure the words were spoken aloud.

Alex closed the lid and stood straight, looking down at her. "The pendant is an original," he said, glancing at his father,

Richard, who had followed Kira out of the back office. Alex threw out a price: "Two-hundred-and-fifty dollars. *For you,* two hundred."

She grinned. "I'm on a reporter's salary. But feel free to give it to Santa Claus, and he can deliver it to me for Christmas."

Alex hesitated. His smile came slowly, creasing the laugh lines around his dark eyes. She listened to the deep resonance of his voice as he explained that he had designed and created the pendant himself under his grandfather's tutelage. Big Bear was a certified jeweler, and Alex, his apprentice. He talked about the design, how he had struggled to arrange the strands of silver to evoke the animal's fur. Kira stared at the necklace, enamored with its detail and delicacy, but more captivated by this unity, this family legacy being shared from one generation to the next.

The bead curtain — separating past from present — tinkled as Big Bear emerged from the back room filling the shop with his presence.

"My eyes are not as good as they used to be and my hands are not as steady, so I don't do it much no more," Big Bear said. "My grandson is a gifted artist. When he puts his mind to it."

Alex rolled his eyes. "I'll never be as good as you, though," he said, returning to his perch behind the counter. Kira moved toward him, but Richard caught her hand, shook it vigorously, and thanked her for listening to their story. His fingers tightened around hers. "If there's anything else, anything at all that we can do, just call."

She assured him she would get in touch soon. Looking at Alex, she said it was nice to meet him, too. He simply nodded. As Kira pulled the door open to leave, the old-fashioned bell tinkling madly, she heard a voice shout, "Wait!" She turned to see Alex coming toward her, waving a page from his sketchpad. "This is for you," he said, handing her a penciled drawing. The page fluttered in the warm breeze. She stared at the image he had drawn of her in her dark pants and sleeveless white shirt, short curls covering her head, hands clasped casually in front. Earlier, she had stood awkwardly in the midst of the shop, awaiting Richard who was in the back on a call with a supplier. Alex had watched her, and now she understood his stare. A small curvy "A" was signed at the bottom. When she looked up to say thanks, he had disappeared inside.

She stared at the picture, an emptiness rising suddenly in her chest. Who was this person in the drawing? Who were *her* ancestors? Her father had been killed in the Vietnam War when she was a baby; beyond that, she knew nothing of him. Her grandfather had been a Baptist preacher, and her mother's grandfather and great grandfather had been farmers. She had never researched her ancestry, preferring to delve into other people's stories. But the interview with Big Bear and Richard Harper had unwrapped a parcel hidden inside her. Their vast historical knowledge awed her. This information had guided them as they grew up; they hadn't needed to research their identity because they knew their stories by heart. By contrast, her family — what was left of it — had lost the art of storytelling. Her mother didn't talk about the past. In the black community, slavery had destroyed many of those historical lines, those family connections that push each generation forward, leaving black families unsure of their origins. Children had been torn from their mothers, fathers sold and shipped off to different plantations, different states. And here, this Native American family, whose history included wars and segregation, reservations and tears, this family had preserved its history. Kira felt a surge of envy for the Harper family — they knew precisely who they were.

3

I WAS BORN in Vauseville, Virginia. My full name is John "Big
Bear" Harper. My grandfather had grown up on the Cherokee
Indian Reservation in North Carolina and had brought his wife and
family to Virginia to live on the land where many of our ancestors
had lived and died. Before the white man came, the Cherokee Nation
was strong and free. We stretched as far north as Ohio and south to
Georgia. Our tribe was in Virginia. We lived in harmony with the
land and the animals that were put on this Earth by the Great Spirit.
We respected them and took only what we needed to survive. Then
Chief Gray Wolf got word that two thousand troops were making
their way to the Cherokee Nation. Families were forced to abandon
their homes. The battle at the Great Island of the Holston River was
a massacre of our people. Despite resistance by the Cherokee warriors,
the troops burned fourteen villages and destroyed crops. There's no
record of how many of our people died. Estimates range in the thou-
sands. Long Arrow's wife, Singing Bird, and their son escaped to
North Carolina. And through her child, Strong Fist, the Harper family line is drawn. Our people made many attempts to return to our
land. Individuals and families trickled back during the nineteenth
century, but the Civil War drove most away again. Still, we came back
to insist on our rightful place here where the Blue Ridge meets the
Alleghenies.

4

A S THE town center faded in her rear view mirror, Kira left behind Suzie's Salon and Tanning Beds, Hall's Quick Mart, The EasyKleen Laundromat, the Bank of Vauseville, and the welcome sign in the median announcing, "A Neighborly Town." Vauseville, Virginia, had grown with the railroad that still thundered its way through the valley, but Kira thought the neon signs detracted from the town's charm. Wooden structures gave way to the trees, flanking her journey back to Fort Lewis. Kira drove her Jeep along the two-lane highway, passing mountains topped with thick forests and fields dotted with horses and cattle. Spring had bloomed across the lush valley, nestled in the southwest region of the state, and in places, the stench of manure filled the air. This part of the region's livelihood came mostly from beef, dairy cows, and Christmas trees. As her thoughts wandered through the scenery, she imagined the Cherokee Indians reigning over this rural landscape.

The front door of Kira's two-bedroom condo opened into a small foyer that led into a living room furnished in soothing tones of beige and brown. This was her refuge and Kira filled it with items that gave her comfort. The framed print of the "Banjo Lesson" hung above the fireplace, a birthday gift from Kenny two or three years ago. She had been taken aback by her brother's thoughtfulness. "That's me," he had said, pointing to the boy on the old man's lap. "I think of me there with Grandpa, jammin on the banjo and having a good old time." Kenny had laughed then, that boyish giggle he had retained from childhood when he had spent hours playing make-believe. She had giggled with him, wishing his dream were true.

She dropped her satchel at the bottom of the staircase, hung her coat in the closet, kicked off her shoes, and then settled onto the couch. She flipped through channels. A cooking show featured a brightly dressed man sprinkling caramelized onions on chicken. A British comedy set in a department store, followed by "The Lawrence Welk Show." She stopped at Bette Davis in "The Letter," and watched the old movie until her eyelids refused to stay open. After eight, she awoke to gunfire in a Western she didn't recognize. Her stomach rumbled, but the kitchen didn't hold much. Standing with the freezer door open, Kira stared blankly into the frosty cavity and wished something delicious would materialize for her dinner. She rested her fingers on a TV dinner — Chicken Alfredo — and looked at a frozen bag of broccoli, a freezer bag of something unrecognizable, and a box of waffles. She stuck the frozen dinner into the microwave.

That had been her life — nothing extraordinary. That was yesterday, the day Kira met Alex. The day before she learned about Larry.

∿

SHE SAT on the couch and poured her fifth drink. The smooth, cold vodka warmed her throat, the heat spreading to her chest and middle. Larry Walsh's number — scribbled by her mother on a scrap of paper — blurred as her eyes lost focus. She took another sip. In retrospect, this day had begun like any other. Although Kira hadn't been able to reach Margaret James, the first woman city manager, whom she wanted to interview for a feature story, an interview with a woman who had published her first children's novel had gone well. In the afternoon, she followed up on her interview with the Harpers by researching the newspaper's archives for information on the local Cherokee Nation.

She had left the newsroom early and stopped at the grocery store. At home, she shuffled around her small kitchen, throwing vegetables together for a salad, and called her mother.

"Oh, Kira. Yes ... hi ... how are you?" Her mother's voice sounded oddly whimsical, distant. Immediately on alert, Kira stopped chopping the celery.

"Sweetheart, I, uh, need to talk to you. Can I come over?"

"Ma, are you okay?" Her mother's heart attack a few years earlier made Kira afraid that it could be happening again. More gently, she asked, "Do you feel all right?"

Her mother's tone was hesitant and unsteady. "I'm fine." Kira was not convinced.

"I can be there in ten minutes," Kira said.

"No. I'm okay, really I am. I just . . ."

Kira waited, pushing back her panic until her mother spoke again.

"I need to run by the pharmacy. Why don't I pick up some chicken for dinner?"

By the time her mother arrived, Kira had piled two plates with lettuce, prepared an assortment of fruits and vegetables, and set out a basket of hard-crust rolls. Her mother placed a box of greasy fried chicken on the table, then stood sucking on her back teeth, staring at the table setting. A warm woman with a smile that softened butter and a voice as thick and slow as cake batter, Martha now stuttered. "I... I got stuck behind this bus—"

Kira watched her — she was always worrying about someone's heart condition or cataract surgery at the senior center where she worked. But instead of sharing her concerns in her usual flood of conversation, Martha fell silent. Gray hairs shimmered through the fading brown dye and shadows made her eyes look tired. Kira scratched an itch at the back of her neck as she pulled out a chair for her mother.

"Sit down, Ma. You want lemonade?"

Martha remained standing, kneading invisible dough between her fingers, and Kira grew more nervous. While she fetched the jug of lemonade for the table, Kira rummaged through her memory for someone who had been sick and may have passed away. She remembered one elderly lady her mother was fond of.

"Is Miss Netta okay?" Using a yellow sponge, she wiped around the plates, forgetting she had cleaned the table earlier.

Her mother's response seemed to come from a distant place inside her. "Her granddaughter's pregnant again. This'll be her third." She kept talking about Miss Netta, but Kira knew something else was on her mother's mind. Still, she waited, letting her talk about the old lady and her family issues. Absently, Kira flung the sponge across the room and it landed back in the sink. She encouraged her mother to sit and eat. Martha mumbled a brief blessing — quick, forced — and using her short nails picked at the skin of the chicken thigh on her plate. They sat quietly nibbling at their food. The next door neighbor's dog gave a burst of wild yapping, rock music blared from a passing car, cubes shifted in the ice-maker. Kira asked again what was wrong. Her mother stared through Kira for several moments.

"I'm not really sure how to tell you." A taut silence lingered too long. "Please don't be angry—"

Kira laid her fork down and swallowed her mouthful of lettuce. She couldn't remember her mother ever being this strange.

"I got a phone call late last night," Martha said. "It was— it was—" She closed her eyes and pursed her lips. The silence expanded, preparing to pop. "It was your father."

Kira blinked rapidly, then tilted her head. Had she heard correctly?

"I know I told you he was dead, but—but he's not." Kira held her breath. "He's in town. He wants to see you." Martha looked away from her daughter's stare. Kira's gaze drifted to the cream vinyl floor.

"He says he's staying here in town for a while. He wouldn't explain why he showed up after all these years. He says he's staying with some friend, although I can't imagine who that is." Martha pushed her plate forward and rested her clasped hands on the table. "I didn't promise anything. I didn't give him your number but got his to give to you."

Kira studied the vinyl flooring — speckles like confetti ranged from beige to almost black. She had never noticed them before.

"I said he was dead, but it just seemed like the best thing to say back then," Martha continued. "I never thought he'd come back."

Kira remembered the photograph she had kept for a long time in a frame on her bedside table, pretending that her father had given it to her. She must have been around eight. Kira fantasized that he had come to visit her, arriving while she slept and awakening her in the dark to present her with a large brown teddy bear with a red plaid ribbon around its neck. In reality, she had cut the picture from an advertisement in an *Ebony* magazine and set it in a frame to make him real. The picture was of a man with light-brown skin like her own, and a coal-black mustache and a short Afro. He held a tumbler in his hand. She had never possessed a real picture of her father; her mother had insisted she didn't have any. Kira had learned not to ask about him either, because her mother had always grown agitated and changed the subject. As a child, Kira had simply let the questions lose themselves inside her.

Now, suddenly, he was alive. The room rocked like an inner tube running through white water rapids, and her mother's words kept floating away.

"He's not dead?"

Her mother shook her head. "I assumed he'd been killed in the war."

How could he be alive, this man she had always believed to be dead? She shook her head. She wanted a vodka and tonic. "I don't understand why you didn't say anything."

"I'm sorry." Her mother's apology slid to the floor. Kira wasn't listening. That her father was alive and wanted to see her spun around her mind, but she couldn't grasp the thought to make it real. Her mother's voice came back to her.

"I didn't think he would ever come back, and I didn't want you to hope that he would. You were so little."

"But I'm grown now, Ma. Why didn't you tell me before now?"

"It was complicated."

"It's not!" Kira felt the heat rise in her face. "What's so complicated about telling me my father is not dead?"

Martha looked pained. Kira pressed the heel of her hand to her forehead, struggling to suppress her anger. Closing her eyes, she struggled to find something good in what was happening. This was an opportunity, a chance to meet her father, to connect with a part of herself she had never known.

"What exactly did he say?" She wanted a complete picture of the man.

"I'd been home a half hour or so when the phone rang. I felt my knees buckle when he said who he was. I didn't believe it at first, but then his voice, well, it sounded so familiar. He asked about you. Wanted to know how old you were now, as if he couldn't figure that out, and what you were doing. I told him about the newspaper job, and he seemed pleased you'd done well for yourself."

"Did he say why he wants to see me? Why now?"

"I asked him that." Martha rolled her eyes. "Said he's been thinking about you for years and only now got the nerve to approach you. Lord, it's been years since we last talked."

"What's he like? I don't even know what he looks like." She wanted to visualize him, but the picture she had clipped from the magazine had faded from her mind. Did she look like him? What would he think of her?

Martha shifted in her seat and looked around the kitchen. "He's—he's not really what you'd expect."

"What do you mean?"

"Well, I never did mention this 'cause it didn't seem to matter. I never thought he'd re-appear in our lives."

Kira stared at her mother, who wouldn't look up from her hands. "What do you mean?"

"Well, he . . ."

"What?"

"He . . . he's not black."

"What!"

"He's white."

Kira felt the blood drain to her feet. She imagined passing out on the floor the way they do in movies and almost willed herself to. Instead, she sat staring beyond Martha, at a blurred image of her mother with a white man, an image she had never, ever contemplated. Her stomach felt as if it was about to heave itself into her throat. She had never envisioned her father as a white man. She was black. Her mother was black. Her brother was black. Everyone she really cared about was black. Her father *had* to be black.

"What do you mean he's white?"

"He's white, Kira. Caucasian. He has white skin." Martha gave a deep sigh. "You make it sound so awful."

"So awful?" Kira said. "First I find out you lied to me my whole life about my father, telling me he was dead, and now you tell me he's alive and wants to see me. And on top of that, you're telling me he's white. It *is* awful. You kept this all a secret. Why would you do that?"

"It wasn't really a secret."

"Then why not tell me?"

"I don't know. It wasn't important."

"Ma, of *course* it's important. This is my father we're talking about. This is about who I am … A white man?"

"You don't have to call him, Kira. He'll understand if you don't want to."

Her mother had slept with a white man, conceived a child, and kept it all hidden. Kira went to the cabinet where she kept the alcohol and poured vodka into a tumbler filled with ice. There had been many lovers, men Kira had taken to bed with few notions of any long-term relationship. But every single one of them had been of African descent. Questions swirled inside her. How did her mother meet a white man and have a relationship with him? Why did he disappear? Who was he?

She sat for a long time thinking about her life, about growing up in a black neighborhood, and seeing the world through black eyes. How her life must contrast with the life of the man who had conceived her!

"You have to tell me the whole story." Kira gulped her drink and took a seat on the couch. Martha leaned back into the cushions and looked around the room. Then, with a sigh, she explained. He had been a trumpet player in a band at a club where Martha — twenty-one at the time — and her sister, Mae, used to go dancing. Underground mixing of blacks and whites in the sixties had been fairly common, and she never thought much about him being white. He was just one of the musicians, sweet and kind. Marriage had never entered her thoughts, nevermind getting pregnant. Having a baby frightened her. When she realized she was carrying his child, she hadn't wanted him to know, but Mae, who wouldn't let anything alone, took it upon herself to tell him.

"He called me, we talked, but then he got shipped out to Vietnam. I figured that was the end of it all."

"You never heard from him again?"

Martha looked away and shook her head.

"He never called or wrote or anything?"

"He did write a couple letters." Her face had lost its dark color. "Actually, he did call me when he got back from Vietnam. But I didn't want him in my life. I told him not to call me again. It was easier to say he had died than to try to be with a white man in the sixties. Those were angry days for mixed couples."

Her mother closed her eyes. She shifted on the couch and pulled a piece of scrap paper from her pocket.

"This is your father's number," she said, placing it on Kira's lap. "His name is Larry Walsh." Martha took Kira's hand and gripped it firmly. "I'd rather not see him, but if you want me around, I'll be there."

Now, Kira sat drinking one glass after another. What did it mean to spend her life without a father and then suddenly learn he was alive and wanted to see her? Who was she now?

5

*A*BOUT TWO-HUNDRED *families make up the Cherokees of the Virginias. Many of them have moved away, but continue to support us. Because the federal government does not recognize the tribe, we can't claim any historical sovereignty to the land, so we decided to raise money to purchase it ourselves, acre by acre. The government says there's no record of a treaty signed, and we've got nothing to prove there ever was one. Our challenge is raising the money before the owners sell it to developers. I'd rather die than see the land destroyed by developers. Old man Newcomb owns most of it. He says he's got Indian blood running through his veins, but he'll only admit that to me. His son's an engineer with some big company up in Fairfax County. Doing pretty well, I'm told, but he's not interested in farming. Then there's Mrs. Foster. Her husband died some years back and she's renting out the land to farmers, but they can't compete no more. She's looking to sell the land to the Forestry Department.*

6

—

A LEX STARED at the gray ceiling wondering how to make his escape. The woman (*what was her name again?*) was stroking his chest and nuzzling his shoulder — getting too comfortable. She had been fun, but he wasn't about to wake up with her in the morning. This was a one-night thing, a few hours, nothing more. He wasn't even sure why he had followed her home. He had driven into Fort Lewis to get away from the same crowd at the local bar. Wanted a quiet drink by himself, time to think. She had started flirting with him, said her date had stood her up. He liked her crooked teeth and bleached blonde hair, but he wasn't planning to see her again. Besides, he wanted to be home before sunrise, before Paw came to open the shop.

He liked living in the studio apartment above the shop. It wasn't where Paw had wanted him to be, but he treasured the freedom of coming and going without his father watching his every move like the hawk Alex had painted on the bedroom ceiling. He painted the bird years ago when he was fifteen and Paw was getting the apartment ready for a family friend who was going to rent the place. Assigned only to paint the walls cream, Alex's mind wandered with the monotony, and suddenly he could see landscapes covering the bare space. He started with long strokes that reflected back to him the hint of feathers. The image of the bird spread through his mind — wings stretched wide across a cloudless sky, piercing eyes scanning the floor for food. He had rushed to the hardware store for gray, black, brown and blue paint. The picture revealed itself to him through the sweeping motion of his arm and the flick of his fingers, appearing above him as if it had always been there, and he was simply uncovering it.

Paw had been mad and in awe all at once. It wasn't often his father was proud of him — or so Alex believed. Richard had said he shouldn't have wasted the time and money on paint, yet described the work as "magnificent." He invited friends and relatives to see it. The tenant, Richard's friend, had photographed it, sending pictures to friends too far away to see it in person. Suddenly, the word "talented" attached itself to Alex's name, and that's when he knew he wanted to be an artist. Except that wasn't the future his Paw or PawPaw had envisioned for him. Richard wanted Alex to go to business school, and then get a law degree like he had. His father wanted him to be like Andrew. But that wasn't Alex. *I don't think Paw really knows who I am.* He almost said the words aloud. Drool from the woman's open mouth slid across his shoulder. Alex gently moved her sleeping head onto the pillow and slipped out of the bed.

Less than five months earlier, Alex had stood in the Fort Lewis bus terminal and shivered, unused to the December cold. The sky was a muted gray, holding back rain or snow, waiting for the right moment to release its weight. The bus driver pulled the bags from the luggage compartment, dropping them haphazardly on the sidewalk. Fumes from the bus made the air rancid. Alex looked around at the mass of people eager to get where they were going for the holiday season and wondered what would happen if he got back on the bus to the Richmond airport and returned to New Mexico. He decided not to dwell on the thought. It wasn't that he didn't want to see his family; in fact, he had felt a rush of excitement as the plane landed. He imagined MawMaw's warm kitchen filled with his favorite desserts: apple pie, sweet potato pie and peach cobbler. He imagined Lorett in her short shorts and tight t-shirts and wondered what it would be like to see her again. He had promised her (she had begged him to promise) that when he got back they would get married. After three years away at school, he was at odds with being home, but he couldn't think of anywhere else to go. He was strapped for money because the construction company had laid him off for the winter, and he couldn't afford any more classes because he refused to ask his father for money. And then there was Gloria — what a mess that turned out to be. Logically, coming home was the best thing to do. It was time to get his real life started, the one he had been delaying: marriage and responsibility. Emotionally, though, he wasn't sure. His father wanted him home, said he needed him to help with the business and with the fundraising campaign. Alex knew his father really meant he needed him to take on responsibilities to lead the clan. Standing on the sidewalk in Fort Lewis, he felt claustrophobic.

"Hey, Geronimo," a boy called. Alex turned. Three pre-teen boys pointed at him. They laughed at his fringed and beaded coat, his long hair and dark skin. The shortest of the three folded his arms and raised his right hand, palm forward. "How!" he said.

Alex scowled at the boys and spat on the ground near their feet. All three took off, laughing and smacking their palms over their rounded lips making whooping noises. He felt disgusted yet not surprised. In Fort Lewis, his long hair often garnered stares and comments, both good and bad. He had spent most of his life being teased about his appearance.

He collected his duffel bag from the ground where the driver had dumped it and went in search of his father. The bus from Richmond had been a half an hour late. Alex spotted his father's truck in the parking lot across the street and as soon as he did, the horn blew and his father descended from the cab. Alex smiled. Richard stood, bow-legged, at the side of the truck. His smile was thin as always and only a few more lines creased his leathery face. Strands of silver fell out from the rubber band that held back most of his hair. Warmth swelled in Alex's chest at the sight of his father, and he dropped his bag by the truck's front tire and hugged him firmly. His father's body had thickened only slightly over the years, and it comforted Alex to feel the familiar frame in his arms.

"Paw. It's good to see you."

"Son." Richard beamed, his palms firm on Alex's shoulders. "Good to see you, too. You look healthy. Your grandma made a feast for your return and here it's not even Christmas Day yet."

As his father gazed at him, Alex suddenly regretted not calling or writing more. He had talked to MawMaw every month or so, sending messages to his father through her, but had called Paw only a few times over the three years. His father wasn't much of a talker; still, he should have made more of an effort. Richard had been angry when he had taken off to New Mexico. Alex was supposed get a business degree and take over the daily operation of the shop while continuing on at school to study law. He was supposed to take on a bigger role with the Committee of Clans and be the community activist his father and grandfather were. While leadership ran through the family line, it stopped dead at Alex.

Richard got back into the driver's seat, while Alex threw his things in the truck bed before getting in beside his father. They drove out of the city and headed west to Vauseville. Alex surveyed the familiar fields, stretched out like dark oceans across the rolling hills dotted with pine trees that, in the cold, were a subdued green waiting for the heat of the sun. The abandoned toll house, a few miles outside Fort Lewis, was still covered in kudzu that looked like brown netting in the winter. Far off, he could see Mr. Newcomb's white mansion like a sentry on the hill. How many times had Alex wondered what it would be like to live in that house, to own all the surrounding land?

"Why you coming home all of a sudden?" Richard kept his gaze on the road ahead, his hands gripping the wheel. Alex thought of Gloria, but that wasn't a story he would tell anyone at home, not even MawMaw.

"I got laid off and no one else was hiring. Just seemed like a good time to come home."

"What about your classes?"

"I still owe them for last semester."

"I'd have sent you money."

"I know." Alex followed the horizon along the gray hills. His father wouldn't call him a failure out loud, but he could feel it in his voice.

"Was it worth it, then?"

"What?"

"Being away, away from us, from the family?"

Alex stared out the window. He didn't want to fight. He was home. Wasn't that enough? He closed his eyes and leaned his forehead against the glass. For three years, he had been immersed in a world of Native American art. On a whim, he had gone to the Institute of American Indian Arts in New Mexico after meeting a student from the school at a Cherokee powwow in North Carolina. The week after the powwow, Alex hopped on a bus to Albuquerque carrying some of his artwork. The school year had already started and classes were full, but the drawing of his brother leaning on his dad's truck caught the attention of Gloria Bennington, who made room for him in her class and persuaded the school to let him register late. "Glorious Gloria," he called her. Muscular legs, skin like porcelain and a smile that weakened his knees. She was a nationally recognized artist who taught him much about his work and himself. She had gladly accepted Alex into her class, her home, and her body. He venerated her. He loved her in a way he could never fully understand and yet to leave her was a relief. But then, having a gun pressed against the side of his head was a considerable incentive to leave.

The truck stopped outside the store where the oldest Harper was waiting for his grandson. Alex stood for a moment and scanned the quiet highway. Birds twittered and a waft of manure stung his nostrils. The storefront looked as it had when he left. The same faded burgundy paint was chipping away from the large window frame. Ginger sat behind the glass cleaning her whiskers, daintily positioned between a tray of necklaces and a sculpture of an Indian chief. PawPaw sat in his old wooden chair at the entrance. Outsiders might view him as an aging relic clinging to the past, but he was chief over the local Cherokee Nation, and in the Indian community, a much-respected man. Alex was proud of him. Big Bear, as he was known, struggled to rise. Alex grabbed his arm to help him up, and then slipped his arms around his grandfather, squeezing him tightly.

"Come, my boy. Talk to me about your experiences."

He followed his grandfather through the shop, into the back room, where Alex had spent many days as a child learning to carve eagles, hawks and a variety of woodland animals from pieces of birch. He could still smell the birch in the air. Sitting on a stool, he shook his head in wonder at all that had happened to him in Albuquerque. "Where to begin, PawPaw? I feel whole, like I've found that part of me that was hidden."

PawPaw settled into a chair and nodded. "It's being at peace with who you are."

"There's so much ignorance here," Alex said, thinking of the boys at the bus station.

"Don't be sad to be home, boy. We've many forlorn younguns here struggling to figure out who they are. You can teach them what you've learned."

"I can try."

"This land is the homeland of our people. Why would we be fighting so hard to claim it back if it meant nothing? We could all travel across the country to New Mexico where Indian culture is alive, but just 'cause it's Indian culture don't make it ours. We are Cherokees of the Virginias. Never forget that." Big Bear poked the air with his forefinger. "You're our future, Alex, and what you do weighs heavy on our family name."

Alex exhaled sharply. The speeches he had left to avoid had begun. Being the last was a burden he would rather not bear. Already, he was growing weary of hearing about the significance of his family name, about the importance of continuing the line, about his responsibilities. As proud as he was of his family, of his grandfather especially, Alex did not want to get stuck in the snare, unable to escape from his family's expectations. Yet, he did want to make them proud of him, and extending the family line was the only way he knew how.

The brass bell that dangled above the store's front door chimed wildly and a woman's voice rang out. "Is he here? Is he back?" Alex heard his father laugh as he tried to calm the woman. Recognizing her voice, Alex took a deep breath and came out from the back office. Lorett stood in the center of the shop, her hair, now shorter, tied into a ponytail. A t-shirt stretched across her chest and a hooded jacket hung loosely about her shoulders. She looked all of fourteen, and his memory jumped back to when they were both teenagers. He saw her running through the forest, hair flapping behind her like a flag in the wind. He was chasing her, trying to pass so she wouldn't win her bet that she could beat him back to the house. Then her giggling gave way to a scream and she tumbled to the ground. When he knelt at her side, her face was covered with tears and blood from a gash along her right temple, and she held what the doctor later announced was a broken arm. Alex had been afraid she would die. In retrospect, his fear had been silly, but at that moment, he had carried her in his arms back to the house asking God not to take her away from him. He had decided then that he loved her more than anything else in the world. And here she was, standing before him, eyes wide and lips parted in a broad smile. "You finally decided to come home, huh?"

He stepped close and touched her cheek, her chin, then ran his fingers along the scar. He felt her stiffen. His trepidation evaporated and he pulled her close, pressing his lips where his fingers had been.

"It's good to see you," he said.

FINALLY DECIDED? Lorett's words echoed through his mind as he walked her back to her mother's house after MawMaw's welcome-home feast. Had he and Gloria not been caught, would he have returned home now? Over the years, Alex and Gloria had grown careless. They had raised eyebrows on campus: they stood a little too close, a little too long, too often. Most nights, Gloria abandoned her sleeping husband and crept downstairs to lay with Alex, claiming that her husband didn't satisfy her anymore. Her husband was often gone for days at a time on business, giving them further opportunity to act on their affections. Their carelessness had spread through her spacious house, and Alex now wondered how long the man had known about their nocturnal (and sometimes daytime) activities. They didn't realize it that Saturday, but Alex and Gloria had made love on the couch in her studio in the rear of the house for the last time. All morning, she had made him stand naked in the middle of the glass room while she painted her image of him in watercolors. Her eyes closed, she had run her fingers across his body before starting — to feel the structure of his muscles, she had said. He laughed. Then she stared at him a long time before placing the paintbrush between her fingers. He begged her for a break, for a chance to lie down. Finally, he flopped onto the couch, and in a moment she was naked too, covering him with her body and her kisses. The sun shone through the tinted glass ceiling as they slept. The click of the revolver wakened him. Gloria's husband grabbed her by the arm and flung her across the floor, telling her to get her clothes on. His voice still echoed in Alex's mind: "Get your fucking red ass out of my house now before I kill you."

In many ways it was a blessing. The intensity of their relationship had shackled him and he couldn't break free on his own. The decision had not been his; nonetheless, here he was back home in Vauseville.

7

KIRA STEPPED off the elevator onto the sixth floor where the news, photo and features departments were located. The opinion columnists were on the floor below, and the floor below that was advertising and marketing. A long reception desk blocked a direct path into the newsroom, a sea of low cubicles with no high partitions for anyone to hide behind. Two television monitors hung from the ceiling so reporters could check local and national news.

She veered right to the features department, where she made a half-hearted effort to clear her desk. Was now the time to call this man, this Larry Walsh, who reportedly was her father? The piece of paper on which her mother had scribbled his number was crumpled from having been repeatedly folded and unfolded. Slouched in her chair, tapping her pen on the pile of papers that cluttered her desk, she wondered whether or not to call. What would she say? *Hello father. Hi dad. Mr. Walsh, this is your daughter.* She looked at the penciled drawing pinned on the corkboard in her cubicle. Alex Harper: A descendant of Cherokee warriors, a family line neatly drawn before African slaves were shipped in shackles to the Americas. While she had no firm, specific knowledge of her ancestors, she had believed they all were rooted in the history of slavery and beyond, hailing from the depths of Africa. But now, only part of her history lay there. In truth, one half of her ancestors could very well have owned the other half. While the thought disturbed her, she was curious to know this mysterious other side.

And what, too, was her mother's story with this man? She scanned her desk, seeing assignments, story ideas, newsletters, magazines she had yet to read, and looked again at the note in her hand. Her finger shook slightly as she dialed the number, and before it rang she hung up. She took a deep breath and dialed again, this time letting it ring, once, twice, three times. A woman answered, "Hello?"

Kira cleared her throat, gave her name, and said she was calling for Larry Walsh. "Is he there?"

"Yeah, wait a minute." The voice was slurred and low. Kira breathed deeply, afraid she would throw up before he answered her call — her morning bagel and coffee churned in her stomach. Then a man's voice spoke on the other end of the line. Panicked, she slammed the phone down, and then left her desk in case he called back. She couldn't do it, couldn't talk to him. Standing in the stairwell with her head in her hands, she felt confused. Life had been fine without him all these years. Why now? As she headed back to her desk a voice stopped her. Beverly was quickly advancing, waving the metro section in the air.

"I'm bringing this up at the next reporters' meeting," Beverly said, stabbing the air with the newspaper. "We always talk about our commitment to producing a . . ." She paused to make a quotations sign in the air with the first two fingers of her free hand, ". . . balanced newspaper, and then they print this."

Beverly shoved the paper in Kira's face. In bold black print, the headline read: "A Community Afraid," and below was a drawing of a black man with a gun. Kira wondered if it had been taken from an old clip art book because of the cartoonish features: the large Afro, the flared nostrils and thick lips. In smaller print next to the drawing were the words, "Community leaders want drugs and guns off their streets." Kira didn't bother reading any more. Beverly was almost panting with fury. "As if the only people who have guns and deal drugs are black," she said.

Kira shook her head in disgust. Little could be done to change the way management liked to operate, and this only proved the status quo would continue. This wouldn't be the first time a story offended blacks; pictures of black men were paraded on the crime page, while the faces of white criminals were excluded, their race hidden behind their names in blocks of print. This disparity was almost a cliché. Kira wondered if she should leave the newspaper. The paper had a diversity initiative that brought in a minority student (usually black) for a three-month stint three times a year. Only one student had been hired out of the program; the girl had stayed only a year before getting snapped up by the *Orlando Sentinel*. In the five years she had been at *The Fort Lewis Times*, Kira couldn't remember any promotions involving black reporters, and no other ethnic minorities had been hired at the paper, at all. Management held only one black editor — Patricia Williams, who oversaw the four weekly neighborhood supplements where subscribers could keep tabs on the school lunch menu and discover the winner of the Bass Fishing Association contest. While the local communities appreciated the news, it was hardly Pulitzer material. Beverly had established a Diversity Committee to look closely at how the newspaper balanced its news and reflected its diverse readership. The committee didn't seem to be making much of a difference, though.

"It makes me so mad," Beverly said. "That's what our committee is for, to stop stuff like this from happening, but they never listen to us."

"Did anyone talk to you about this story before it went to print?"

Beverly's forehead wrinkled. "Are you kidding? I hope they're not planning to run this picture again. We should have a committee meeting to talk about it."

8

*O*UR PEOPLE *are only now growing strong again and regaining the pride they once had. Our people were forced to attend black schools because the government wouldn't spend money on another separate school system for us Indians. We weren't allowed to have our own identity. In fact, there was a law that classified all Indians as black. Those who could pass for white shed themselves of their culture and turned their backs. Blacks didn't understand why we didn't want to attend their schools. It wasn't that we didn't want to associate with them; it was because we wanted our own culture. We didn't want to be black, we wanted to be Indian, but that's not easy to explain in a world where people judge each other so heavily on color and religion. I helped organize an Indian school here in Vauseville that taught us pride in who we are. It was closed, of course, in the early sixties when desegregation hit this area. But the building is still standing. It's our community center now. We're trying to fill it with our history. We have a few items in there already, pots, arrowheads, things that were found around here.*

9

—

KIRA SPENT the morning at the library researching local Cherokee history, losing herself in the musty smell of old books, which contained more about the assortment of generals who fought the "wild savages" than about any Cherokee warriors. She caught herself thinking about Alex, imagining his hair whipping behind him as he crossed the landscape on horseback. Stereotypical, she knew, but whimsical and seductive, too. She couldn't help it that his classical Native good looks inspired daydreams that took her to the Old West where he swept her away into the wild. A chuckle escaped her and she mouthed an apology to the elderly gentleman frowning at her over his newspaper. As she read about the battle at the Holston River, her lips parted slowly in awe when, there on the page, staring back at her with stern eyes, was a sketch of Chief Gray Wolf, whose story Big Bear had recounted. Seeing his picture made the story all the more real. The great chief sat with his hands resting on his lap, keenly focused on the artist drawing his likeness. Kira made a photocopy of the page and carefully placed it in a folder to take back to the Harpers.

BIG BEAR sat in his usual spot at the door, this time carving a woodpecker. On her first visit to the shop he had been shaping the head of a pipe. She had parked her Jeep on the street outside the little store, which, with its log cabin design, looked appropriate for the quaint town nestled in the green hills. The words "Big Bear's Cabin" were carved into a wooden plaque above the doorway. A ginger cat had been stretched out in the bay window, enjoying the heat passing through the glass. The slight flick of its tail, the only indication the cat was alive.

"Nice Jeep," said Big Bear.

Kira was about to say thank you when she realized she had arrived in her Cherokee Sport. She blushed and kicked herself for not making the connection before now. Embarrassed, she laughed and tried to shrug it away.

ON HER second visit, the cat still lay in the same position in the window. Kira stood on the sidewalk watching the old man seated at the entrance on a wooden chair. Big Bear's long gray hair was tied back in a skinny ponytail, a few wisps dangling over his forehead. His golden-brown skin was smooth.

"Came back, huh?" he said, without raising his eyes. She nodded and he grunted.

"What are you working on today?"

"Same as every day." He continued flicking his penknife and shards of wood spun away and landed at his feet.

"And what's that?"

"Working on how to make it through another day without getting into trouble."

Kira grinned. As if handling a relic, she pulled the page from her satchel and presented it to him. Big Bear stopped carving and looked at her. He held the page close to his face and squinted at it. "Well, ain't that something." She explained that she had found a book in the library that featured the drawing. Big Bear stood up in a way that made Kira want to catch his arm; his movement was unsteady to anyone who didn't know his aging body had its own way of moving. He shuffled into the shop and called out to his son, "Lookee here at what the reporter brought."

Richard came from behind the counter and took the page from his father as Big Bear recounted where it had come from. Richard shook his head in awe. "I've never seen a picture of him before, have you, Paw? We've got some pictures from years back, but none of Gray Wolf. And they had this in the library? This is great." He took her hand and shook it firmly.

When she asked after Alex, Richard disappeared into the back office and called upstairs to his son, whose voice boomed back that he was busy. Richard's face appeared through the beads, telling her to go up. Kira shook her head, not wanting to intrude, but Richard nudged her toward the stairs, shouting upwards: "It won't take long." He looked at Kira and smiled, urging her on.

She climbed the narrow creaky stairway. The top opened into a spacious studio-styled apartment with dull wooden flooring. Gone were the tomahawks, dream catchers and drums sold to the tourists downstairs. In their place were statues and paintings of Native Americans wearing jeans and t-shirts. To Kira, their ordinariness seemed unusual. On the wall at the top of the stairs, hung an oil painting of a man wearing overalls and leaning proudly against a steam engine. Only his brown skin and long dark hair gave away his heritage. The man could have been Alex, but most likely it was Big Bear in his younger years. Near the back wall, the youngest Harper sat at a flattened artist's table, diligently working on a statue that stood in the middle of wood shavings. She said hello. Alex looked up and welcomed her with a broad grin that softened his hard features. An unanticipated knot twisted at the base of her stomach and her teeth clamped down on the inside of her cheek — she had forgotten how striking he was. His hair hung loosely over his shoulders and his smoky eyes were almost hidden by dark lashes. He leaned back in his chair and she thought he could have been the creation of his own hands.

"Miss Franklin, it's a pleasure to see you again. It is Miss, right?"

"Yes, it's Miss."

"So, what do I have to do for you?"

"*Have* to do? You don't have to do anything," she said, strolling toward his corner.

"Oh, yes I do. My father sent you up here and expects me to be nice to you. He's eager to get a good story in the newspaper."

She strolled over vibrant rugs strewn across the wooden floor and passed a soft black leather couch that looked as though it would suck her deliriously into the center of the earth. The room was sparsely furnished; each piece emanated a subtle sensuality, from the couch to the curvy pots scattered along the edges of the room, to the figurines she guessed had been created by Alex. Next to his worktable stood a heavy wooden chair with an ornate back. Studying the wood for a second, she realized an eagle was carved into the top of the chair. Running her fingers over the smooth grain, she asked if it was his work. Alex nodded, his fingers lightly touching a statue on the table before him.

"I could just watch you work and you wouldn't have to say anything. Your father wouldn't know if you'd been nice to me or not."

"Will it affect the story?"

"Perhaps."

"Let me think about that." Alex leaned forward and used a miniature carving knife with a straight pointed blade to form the statue's face. Kira stood in silence watching him chip away specks of butternut to etch a nose. His long fingers gripped the blade and she noticed his skin had thickened and hardened in places where he had likely nicked himself. The creamy statue depicted a Native American woman standing about a foot tall with feathers carved into her hair, but instead of a traditional Indian dress, she wore a flowing gown blown backwards by Alex's imaginary wind. Kira began to feel awkward in the silence but let him work. She looked at the shelf that ran almost the entire length of the sidewall below a series of windows that washed the room with light.

"I'm sure you have a list of questions," he said. "Go ahead and ask them."

Nodding at the figure in front of him, Kira asked, "What's that you're working on?"

"A statue."

"I mean, who is she?"

Alex pondered the question, then said theatrically, "She is the spirit of love who comes to me every night."

"Well, aren't you lucky! Does she have a brother who would visit me?"

Alex chuckled. "No, no brother. . . . Perhaps a cousin. I'll find out for you."

Kira turned again to the shelf. At one end stood another figurine of a woman, this one carved from dark, almost black wood.

"So who's this," she asked. "The spirit of evil?"

"Maybe. She comes to me as well and torments me."

"Why is it that everything black has to be evil?" Kira looked more closely at the figure and noticed the round flat nose and thick lips. Surprised by her discovery, she turned to Alex. Concentrating on his new creation, he seemed to ignore her. "She really is black."

"That doesn't make her evil," he said. "If she torments me to drive me crazy, then she's evil. If she torments me because she loves me, then she's crazy."

"Why a black woman?"

Alex leaned back in his chair and shrugged. "Why not? That's what I saw in the mahogany. An African woman."

She studied him, ever more intrigued. "Did she really come to you in a dream?"

"Why would I lie?"

Kira frowned and wondered if he was teasing her again, but his straight face gave away nothing. She took pleasure in sparring with him. "So, are these nightmares you're having, or fantasies?"

Alex laughed a deep laugh that roused a tingle at the base of her spine. "I don't think she's evil. But her torment is mine and not to share with you." He fixed a stare on Kira and she looked at the floor then turned away. Why was it that in the same moment she wanted to slide into a hole in the floor to escape his stare, she also wanted to dive into those black eyes and swim through his thoughts? He lowered his eyes and returned to work. Looking at the items on his shelf, she noticed a boy's clay face, which was mask-like, except the eyes were filled in. The features were reminiscent of Alex. On the wall behind the mask was a penciled drawing of what could have been the same boy standing on an upturned bucket, leaning into the engine of an old Ford truck. The paper had browned slightly and the edges were curled. The boy's face was grubby and he was grinning from ear to ear.

"Are these of you?"

"No." Alex continued to work.

Kira waited for an explanation and when he remained silent she asked who the boy was. Alex raised his head and stared at the mementos on his shelf. He laid the knife on the table and said, "My brother."

A tightness in his throat hinted at some tension with his sibling. She hesitated before asking if he lived in Vauseville near the rest of the Harper family. Alex paused before answering. "He died of pneumonia when he was sixteen. He was my older brother."

"I'm so sorry." Kira looked at the young boy's face in the drawing and imagined Alex looking this way as a child. "He was very beautiful," she said. She felt Alex's stare but didn't look around. He responded with a quiet thank you, then cleared his throat and said that his brother would have been twenty-seven this year. His name was Andrew.

"We would have been about the same age," she said. "You must miss him?

He shrugged and began to fiddle with the wood chips lying around the statue. "We were planning to escape out West and become professional Native dancers and travel the world." The glimmer of a smile radiated across his face. "He could build cars out of nothing. PawPaw, my grandfather, had this old truck, the one in the picture, and Andy said that as soon as he got it fixed we'd hit the road. He never did fix the old thing."

"And you never got away."

He nodded slowly, his hair shifting like an enchanted adder on his shoulder. She leaned on the back of the wooden chair; now it was her turn to scrutinize him.

"I got away, but my home never got away from me. When Andy died, I became the last of our clan. Paw's last hope, if you will."

"The last hope?"

"The only son."

She realized he was talking about grandchildren and noted his lack of enthusiasm.

"Everyone has to come home eventually," he said.

"Are your parents divorced?"

He jabbed the knife into the table. "My mother's dead, too."

The blunt statement shocked Kira into silence. She chose not to dig for more information about his mother's death, at least not today. Turning back to the shelf, she pulled forward a framed photograph of a young woman with an earthy appearance and crow-black hair resting over her shoulders. A scar ran from her right eyebrow almost to her cheek. As if anticipating her question, Alex answered. "That's Lorett, my . . . uh, fiancée, I guess."

"You guess?"

"It's still new."

Kira silently acknowledged the woman's attractiveness and returned the picture to the shelf. "I never did see this land y'all are trying to buy. I know you're busy, but would you show it to me?"

He studied the statue. "Sure. Why not? You've already broken my concentration."

He disappeared through what Kira had thought to be a closet door As she approached, she realized it was a bedroom. White sheets lay crumpled on the double bed. A dressing table and drawer unit filled the small room. A light shone from an attached bathroom where Alex scrubbed his hands. An image on the ceiling caught her eye: a large bird, its wings reaching to each corner of the room.

"Did you do that?" she asked.

"Yeah," he said, passing her in the doorway and heading for the stairs. "C'mon."

His father's old black truck was parked next to Kira's Jeep. "Yours?" He nodded toward her vehicle.

"Don't say a word," she said. "Your grandpa already embarrassed me enough." Alex laughed.

They drove for about ten minutes along a winding paved road lined with oak trees and pines. The sun followed them and Kira felt sweat trickle down her back and moisture collect in the creases of her eyelids. She dabbed her eyes with her t-shirt sleeve. With the truck's windows down, the warm air swirled around their heads as they chatted about the unusually warm weather. Every few miles the trees cleared revealing farmhouses and pastures with cattle. Alex pointed out the elementary and high schools and the town's oldest church.

"You see that building there?" Kira followed his finger pointing to a large two-story brick building with high windows, back a little from the road. "That's our community center. PawPaw and my father bought it and fixed it up. They worked on it almost a year. Folks around here volunteered their time to get it renovated. They painted the inside, repaired the roof and put in a new furnace. It really brought folks together."

"How old is it?"

"It was built around 1850, I think, as a school, and sat empty for years till my folks turned it into a community center. The seniors' club meets there and there's a kids program on weekends. It's not just us Indians who use it."

Us Indians. Kira had noticed the Harpers referred to themselves as Indians, not as American Indians or Native Americans, the politically-correct names outsiders, like herself, used. The word seemed too simple, too vague, and didn't capture the depth of the people. But the same could be said for the term "black" instead of African American. She scribbled a few observations about the building and the countryside they were driving through. After slowing the truck, Alex made a sharp left turn onto a dirt road barely wide enough for two vehicles to pass each other. The road wound its way through thick trees. About three miles in, he parked on the grassy shoulder and said they would walk about a quarter mile through the trees. "Can you make it?"

Kira cut her eyes at him and replied, "Do I look that frail?"

He smirked and turned up a dusty path that led into the woods. They walked along a trail dotted with deer tracks, ferns and pinecones. Kira wished she had worn sneakers instead of open-toed sandals but wasn't about to complain. Birds chattered in the trees announcing the presence of intruders. High branches blocked the stifling heat of the sun, making it pleasantly cool. When the forest began to thin, Kira heard the rush of water and realized she was being led to a river. The woods made way for a clearing at the river's edge, dotted with weeds and patches of grass. Large rocks slowed the water's flow, creating small pools perfect for wading. Kira resisted the urge to dip her feet. Alex crouched onto his knees and put his hand into the water as if testing the temperature. His movements were smooth and deliberate.

"This is Deer Creek." He cupped his hand and brought water to his mouth. Kira watched him with his head bowed, eyes closed, lips kissing his palm, oblivious to the water dripping from his chin and hand. As he stood and flicked his head, his hair floated away from his face. A man of color, although his skin was a shade or two lighter than hers, his features more white than black. His distinctive Native American culture and history placed him firmly within his own race. Kira had never envisioned herself finding a lover outside her own people, but she found Alex almost irresistible. A man so different, a man not of her race. Was that her mother's attraction to Larry Walsh?

She followed his gaze to the other side of the river, where the woods had been cleared to reveal pastures of green that ambled for miles. On the horizon were the whispery blue Allegheny Mountains. The panorama rendered Kira silent. In all her years in Fort Lewis, she now realized she had never taken time to stand in the glory of its scenery and appreciate the warm, fresh air. A haze had settled over the mountains and the sun was strong. Alex described the location of the land his people were attempting to reclaim. It started where they had parked and ran across the river for about thirty miles and north for another fifty. They stood admiring the view. Kira looked at her companion; he seemed entranced. She started to speak but decided to wait, to let him think. As she listened to the birds' chatter, tranquility fell over her like a veil.

"I can't imagine living here, having all this space," she whispered, afraid to break the peace yet unable to contain her wonder.

"This land defined who we were," Alex said, picking up a flattened stone. He skimmed it over the river's surface where it skipped twice before falling with a plop.

"So all this belonged to the Cherokees?"

"This and much, much more. The Cherokee Nation extended from the Ohio River down to Georgia. There were twenty-five thousand of us reigning over all that land. Can you believe that? That's going back to the 1700s, mind you."

Kira found it hard to imagine all the farmland, separated now by fences and property lines, spanning out as one landscape. Alex seemed to lose himself in the glitter of the river before chucking another rock into its depths.

"Farmers own the land now, right?"

"Mostly, but developers have their eye on it. The farmers have gotten old and are looking to sell."

"My grandfather was a farmer," she said. "He grew cotton and tobacco, I think, but big business forced him out. I bet a lot of blacks lost their land around here."

Alex folded his arms across his chest, resting his foot on a boulder. "This was our land before it was anyone else's. This land was stolen from us, and now we're struggling to raise money to buy it back."

"Yes, but blacks struggled to survive here, as well. That was my point."

Alex didn't seem to hear her. "Everything you see once belonged to my people, and bit by bit it was taken away and we were forced onto reservations, as if the land had belonged to white folks all along. This land was our life."

"I know. It's so unfair."

"But you don't know," he said, staring across the landscape, his voice so low Kira strained to hear his words. "You don't have a clue about how we feel. You think you do. You think because . . ." He checked himself and fell silent.

"What?" Kira stepped closer, challenging him to continue. She wanted to hear what he was hiding under his silence, but he shook his head. "Because what?" she insisted.

He narrowed his eyes, a slight wrinkle creasing his forehead, watching her like a security guard in an expensive department store, as if he knew her kind. He spoke soft and slow at first, and then, like a train coming out of the station, he picked up speed and thundered forward. "You think because you're black you understand all the hardships of the world. Black people are spoiled. You turn everything around so that it's all about you."

"I didn't mean it like that." She wanted to explain that she sympathized with his cause, that she understood, that her mother's father had experienced tough times because of white developers as well. "Black farmers have had it rough," she said. "They don't get the financing they need and end up owing so much money they can't survive. Like my grandfather. He lost his farm when my mother was a child because he couldn't compete with the bigger white businesses."

"But *we* were the first people," he said. "Ani Yunwiya. This was our land. Our country. And then here you come along, talking about your rights and your freedoms and suddenly everyone notices the injustices."

He turned to her and his stare burned deeply. She felt unjustly accused, but couldn't respond — where had the sculptor gone who had created the image of a beautiful African woman? She kept silent, pressing her tongue behind her lower teeth as he continued. The urge to run, to escape his words, clouded her thoughts, though she stood, hoping he would stop. He kept on berating the world for not supporting his people.

Finally, with her heart pounding in her ears, she spoke. "Now wait one damn minute." Alex's head jerked around to look at her. "You think that because this was once your land no one else can understand the pain of losing it? Do you have any idea what my ancestors went through? They were stolen from their land, never to see it again." Kira was shaking but faced him down. "Our freedoms were not handed to us on a silver platter. People like my grandfather and his parents before him fought hard to own their own farms. To finally reap some reward from land they had once toiled as slaves. I may not have been there, and I may not have a direct link to my ancestors like you do, but I sure as hell know of the suffering blacks endured serving their white masters."

He blinked rapidly and his eyes clouded behind his lashes. He studied her as he had done before, but this time she fought the urge to look away. She stared him down. Eventually, Alex lowered his eyes and watched the flies dance on the water.

"I didn't mean to take this out on you," he said. "Sometimes I get frustrated by so many things. At the responsibilities heaped on each generation to get back what we should already have." He glanced at her.

"Isn't getting back this land a start?" She watched him and waited. His mouth opened but he said nothing. His angry expression had all but disappeared and he closed his eyes for a moment before looking at the sky.

"It's late." He turned quickly and headed down the path toward the truck. Kira struggled to grasp what had just transpired, yet felt oddly elated by the discussion. There was something frightening, yet invigorating, about Alex Harper. Before hurrying after him, she scribbled what she could remember of his words in her notepad. She thought she would catch him, but his stride was longer and he already sat in the truck. She pulled on the heavy door and climbed inside the cab. His hands rested on the wheel and he peered sideways at her. "I didn't mean to attack you back there." He swallowed. "I don't know what came over me. I just . . . I'm sorry."

"It's okay, really. It's probably good for you to let it out." She smiled, somewhat relieved. "Although I wish I hadn't been the target, it helps me understand where you're coming from. I can't write an honest story if I don't understand what you're feeling. I'm not going to say I know all about your people, and I don't expect you to know all about mine. But we should come together because of our struggles instead of separating ourselves and fighting."

Nodding in agreement, he started the engine. "You're not going to print all that are you, you know, what I said back there?"

Her smile broadened. "Maybe."

Alex glowered. They traveled back in silence, and Kira wondered if she could ever understand his pain. She could make speeches about the complexity of human nature and pontificate about people's struggles, but could she honestly understand the perspective of an Indian man living with the weight of his family's historical significance? What was it like to look out at a land that once belonged to your ancestors — ancestors who could be traced back three centuries, whose names and faces you knew? Ancestors who'd had the freedom to wander through the countryside without crossing someone else's property or being stopped by a fence — that freedom was incomprehensible to her.

She remembered the tiny yard behind her mother's house where she and Kenny raced their bicycles in a circle, going round and round. No trees or shrubbery, just thin grass where they had made their racetrack. That was their freedom. No wide-open spaces, just the busy street on the other side of the fence. Indoors, the living room window represented their movie screen to the world. Kenny sat in that front window crying out at the top of his lungs the names of the cars that passed by. How he had irritated Kira, yet she sat with him, watching the pretty high-school girls wearing the latest fashions and hairstyles. How she had wished she could be just like them — outside, laughing and having fun instead of inside babysitting her brother. In her mind, she was speeding away in one of those fancy cars to somewhere exotic and exciting. That was her freedom.

10

HIS GRANDMOTHER, Elaine Harper, had a way of knowing what was on his mind. Sometimes Alex liked it because she would ask him questions and get him to talk about things he wasn't sure how to talk about. Other times it annoyed him how she dug for information he wasn't willing to share. This time, he wanted to talk, but didn't know how to get started. His outburst earlier with the reporter embarrassed him and he couldn't fathom what had brought on the strong feelings that grabbed him then. He wasn't the activist his father wanted him to be, yet there he was spouting rhetoric about his ancestral history. Perhaps his years in New Mexico had made a deeper impression on his psyche than he had imagined. The Indian culture was entrenched in the Southwest because of the numerous tribes there, making cultural pride a given. He had enjoyed being among Indians from all across the country, studying at the university. Back in the Fort Lewis–Vauseville area, people didn't much care about the local Indians. Alex felt cheated knowing how different life could be for his people.

"Don't rub the pattern off the plate, Alex," said Elaine. "I think it's dry enough you can put it on the shelf now."

He looked at the dinner plate in his hand. For as long as he could remember, dinner at his grandmother's meant helping her clean up the kitchen after eating. She frequently complained that she didn't know how her son had grown up to be so helpless in the home, and she was determined her grandsons would know how to help their future wives with the housework. As a result, the boys had found themselves drying dishes and wiping the table after dinner. He carefully placed the plate in the cupboard and took another off the draining rack.

"It sure is good to have you around again," she said.

He dried the dish and grabbed a cup.

"You ought to bring Lorett over for dinner one evening. I ain't seen much of her since you announced your engagement. You're not regretting nothing, are you?"

He shook his head even though he knew she couldn't see him; her attention was focused on scrubbing a pan. He didn't know how to say he felt confused and unsure, rushed and yet glad to be forced to settle down. He had a vision of himself married, living in a big house with five kids running around him, a pretty wife with her belly bulging with another child — both of them happy. That's what marriage should be. Not what it had been for his father. The reporter had asked about his mother — she was a shadow he couldn't touch, a question he couldn't answer. Had her marriage really been so miserable that she couldn't prevail? Were her sons so meaningless that she never considered their loss? He couldn't make his vision of marriage real. Kept running instead of staying put. But then, maybe it wasn't him in the picture. The wife and the kids had always been Andy's destiny, not Alex's.

His grandmother stopped scrubbing and looked at him. "You ain't thinking of someone else, are you?"

"No!" he said, a little too quickly. Four months had passed since New Mexico, and with each new day, Gloria fell farther and farther behind him. He had to let her fade away, but in her place he wanted someone who thrilled yet calmed him, who intrigued and motivated him the way she did. Lorett couldn't fulfill that role and he knew it was unfair to expect her to. Besides, what good was there in trying to repeat something that had been flawed from the start?

"It's kinda scary taking vows to be with one person for the rest of your life," he said.

Elaine dried her hands on her apron, poured lemonade for two and led him to the front porch where they sat on the wooden swing that creaked with age.

"Marriage ain't to be taken lightly," she said. "I know your father's eager to see grandbabies, but don't let him shove you into this if you ain't ready. We don't need another mess of a marriage."

"It's time, though, don't you think?"

"It ain't what I think, Alex."

"It's what Andy would've done," he said. He felt the weight of his brother. His dutiful brother who talked and talked about leaving but would have stayed, married a good woman, and extended the family with countless children. Andy would have been a great leader. He had been the captain of the debate team, the lead rusher on the football team, and would have gone on to be the lawyer Paw had dreamed of. When Andy died, all eyes had turned to Alex, who hated sports, hated talking in front of people, hated responsibility. Why couldn't he just roam the country, dancing and sculpting?

"Do what's right for you," Elaine said.

The problem that seemed to be growling at his feet, however, was that he didn't know what was right for him. One thing he knew for certain: he was tired of running.

"What would Maw have wanted? What would it be like now if she hadn't—"

"Don't." Elaine patted his hand and squeezed his fingers. Looking at the wooden beams below her feet, she said, "Your Maw had troubles, Alex, troubles nobody could understand or solve. She's gone and we can't sit here wondering what life would be like if she was still here. Live for today and move confidently into tomorrow. Don't look back and wonder why."

But he did wonder why. He feared that what happened to his father could happen to him, as well.

On Christmas Day, he had seen the expectation in Lorett's eyes that her gift would be an engagement ring, then heard the flat "Oh wow," followed by "What a surprise," when she opened his gift to find a sculpture he had made of her as a little girl. Nor did he miss her disappointment at the New Year's celebration in the community center when he gave no surprise announcement at midnight. As teenagers, they had talked about getting married after high school, except when the high of graduation had faded, Alex couldn't imagine being a married man, and becoming a father seemed all the more alien. He had promised her that she would one day be his wife, but explained his desire to travel with a Native dance troupe first. Lorett vowed to wait for him, no matter how long.

On the January evening Alex planned to propose, he turned to his grandmother. He peered into the kitchen where she was mashing sweet potatoes for a pie. His grandfather sat snoring on the La-Z-Boy by the fireplace in the sitting room.

"What you making?"

"Dinner ain't ready yet," she said, without looking up.

His grandmother had a chicken in the oven and fresh green beans simmered in a pot. He wanted to take a seat at the table and remain there instead of heading out.

"I can't stay. I'm taking Lorett to dinner."

"You fixin to ask for her hand?" She stopped and looked at his face. He looked at the floor. "Nervous? That's natural. You got her a ring?"

Alex took the box from his pants pocket, flipped it open and revealed a quarter-carat marquis diamond. Elaine wiped her hands on her apron, took the ring and squinted at it under the dimming light. "Put the big light on so's I can see it better." Her eyes widened in admiration and she nodded approval. "You bought this all by yourself? She'll love it." She hugged his neck and told him he had done good. Alex sighed with relief.

"You ready?" she asked.

"MawMaw, to be honest, I really don't know."

She chuckled. "No one's ever truly ready for marriage and making families, but don't let folks rush you. You take more time if you need it."

"It's time. She's been waiting for this a long while." He hugged his grandmother again, kissing her soft cheek. "Save me some pie."

AS HE sat in the restaurant, the ring felt like lead in his pocket. He couldn't decide whether his rapid pulse meant he was exhilarated or afraid. Perhaps both. He raked his fingers through his loose hair and moved the vegetables around on the plate with his fork. Lorett appeared to glow in the dim light and he acknowledged her beauty. He still loved her and wanted to make her happy — he just wasn't sure that he could. He could tell she knew something was wrong with him that evening. Her head tilted and he watched her hair swing away from her face on one side and cling to her cheek on the other. It made her look like an innocent little girl. He smiled weakly. They talked about the restaurant, how classy it was, how expensive. She wanted to know what the special occasion was, why all the extravagance? He shrugged. "Why not? A beautiful woman like you deserves a little extravagance now and then." The waiter brought Lorett her dessert and Alex watched her dip her spoon into the chocolate mousse. He knew that she knew why. They sat in silence while she savored the sweet dish. He took a deep breath to speak. He had practiced what to say in front of the mirror while shaving, on the way over to her mother's house to pick her up, and driving into Fort Lewis. He had said it over and over in his mind, and now the words just wouldn't come. But he *would* propose. He would marry her and make her happy, and fulfill the role his brother should have played.

"Are you all right?"

Alex looked up from the table. "I'm fine. Let's go. Are you finished?"

Lorett giggled. "I've eaten so much I can't move. I think I'm going to have to ride in the bed of the truck after you roll me out of here."

The waiter had left the check but was taking too long to return so Alex left cash on the table including a generous tip. He took the long route back to Vauseville through the winding country roads. As they rose into the mountains, into the darkness, the city lights blurred behind them. Lorett linked her arm around his and clung to him for the entire half-hour drive to her house, as if to avoid any chance he would escape. He steered the truck into the yard and

Lorett remained seated in the truck when he cut the engine off, waiting for him to come around and open the door for her. He had forgotten how this irritated him — Gloria had never waited for him to open doors for her even though he would have gladly carried her across every threshold she encountered. An upstairs light was the only sign of life in the house. He knew they wouldn't go inside. Lorett's mother disliked her daughter having male visitors late at night.

Standing on her mother's porch, Alex swallowed the lump in his throat and got down on one knee. The night air was crisp and a cool wind made him shiver. He tugged at the collar of his jacket. Snow would fall again tomorrow.

"Lorett . . ." She stared at him, an excited, eager smile on her face. She knew the words already, knew his intention. For a split second his mind went blank. Where were the words? He reached into his jacket pocket for the ring. He froze. It wasn't there. Then he remembered he had tucked it into his pants pocket.

"Lorett," he repeated, feeling his throat closing and his heart vibrating wildly in his chest. "Will you—will you be my wife?"

Her eyes bulged. Instantly, she grabbed the ring and slipped it on her finger. "It fits perfectly." He stood up and her arms wrapped around his neck, "yes" echoing in his ears. She burst into tears and he held her as they sat on the porch steps. His chest felt heavy and his shoulders tight. She rambled on about having a huge wedding in the spring, wearing her grandmother's dress, inviting everyone in the community, her cousin making the cake, building a house and starting a family as soon as the house was finished.

"The last of the Harpers is getting married," she said.

He smiled but felt woozy from the reality of the proposal. Her words were suffocating him. Finally, he told her spring was too soon. They would get married next year. He squeezed her hand. "We can plan to spend our wedding night in our new home. And I promise, on that night, we'll start our family. Okay?"

"Our family." She kissed his cheek. "Oh Alex, that sounds wonderful."

"Yeah." He closed his eyes.

More than anything, he wanted to be in Albuquerque. He wanted Gloria. He wanted to be wrapped in her arms. With her, he was just an artist — there were no obligations, no promises, and no expectations.

11

S HE SMEARED dark red over her lips. As she looked in her bedroom mirror, Kira was caught again by that disconnect between her reflection and what she felt inside. Chocolate brown eyes decorated with bright colors and painted lashes. High cheekbones dusted with rouge. She was tired. Tired of playing these stupid dress-up games, making herself pretty so men would adore her. Some nights, all she wanted was to stretch out and sleep with her arms around a warm body — someone permanent. Yet somehow she had surrounded herself with men who loved her looks, men who weren't looking for conversation or anything permanent. Kira knew how to make a man desire her. She played the game well. But what was supposed to happen after the passion ended?

She stepped back from the wall mirror. Her black dress was a nylon-lycra blend with pencil straps and a plunging neckline. Jamal had bought it for her earlier that day at the mall. The dress hugged her hips and crept up her thighs as she twisted and turned — a trinket to catch a man's eye. She sighed. At some point on her career path her notion of changing the world had fallen through a grate along Main Street. She had envisioned herself managing a newsroom in New York or Los Angeles, not floundering in the features department at a rural city paper. She had imagined herself married to a lawyer espousing justice on the six o'clock news, not casually seeing a junior executive only interested in her body.

The car horn announced Jamal's arrival, so she slipped her toes into leather high heels, covered her shoulders with a gray shawl, and answered her man's summons. They sped through the side streets of Fort Lewis — streets that had once been main thoroughfares with corner stores, barber shops and diners but, with the city's growth, were now forgotten. Warehouses sat empty and boards covered broken windows of what used to be flourishing shops. The city's downtown was in the midst of a redevelopment project and already boasted restaurants, coffee shops and bookstores oozing with artsy pseudo-riche customers from the suburbs. Boutiques with hand-made cards and jewelry selling at exorbitant prices dominated the main streets. But the back roads, lined with peeling front porches held up by a prayer, went unnoticed — until someone was murdered. Then a TV news reporter flashed the nearest cross-streets on the evening news. Her mother still lived on those streets, where Kira had grown up. She had skipped over the cracked pavements, played double-dutch and hopscotch in the middle of the road, moving to the side when a car came by. She had ridden her bike through the side streets imagining herself a sophisticated detective seeking clues to an atrocious killing. She had chased her little brother and then hidden from him until his yells were unbearable, forcing her to reveal herself from behind a neighbor's hedge before someone called the police. Kira frequently felt a twinge of guilt for moving to the suburbs where the mostly white, soon-to-be upper class were transitioning to the big homes farther out of town near the golf course. Some might say she had turned her back on her roots, but Kira simply wanted to find somewhere to breathe.

With Jamal's swift driving, they arrived at the hotel in under thirty minutes. Kira loosely held Jamal's arm and used her free hand to smooth the hemline that stopped halfway down her thigh. She wobbled slightly on the hardwood floor as they stepped into the hall. She smiled, quietly acknowledging the admiring glances from Jamal's male work friends and taking pleasure in their attention. Jamal adjusted his tie. His look would fit comfortably on the cover of a magazine, she thought. He was lanky but muscular and never wore the same suit and tie twice in one week. His skin was cherry-wood brown and his hair cut military-style — she loved the velvety feel of his hair as she ran her fingers down and how it prickled when she ran her fingers upward. She had met him more than a year ago waiting for the elevator in the Markus office building. He had looked stunning in a dark brown suit that complimented his skin tone. He carried a black briefcase that matched his soft leather shoes. They eyed each other discreetly around the others filling the elevator. As she exited, he said, "Excuse me, ma'am. You have a run in your pantyhose." Kira paused to look at her leg but found no run. By the time she looked up, he was holding his business card out to her. His originality instantly appealed to Kira.

Standing inside the hall, now, he flicked an invisible piece of lint from his tweed jacket and kissed her earlobe before letting her go to shake a co-worker's hand.

The cocktails were fine, the chicken moist and the music a mixture of country, Top Twenty pop and golden oldies. Kira stifled a yawn. Another of Jamal's work functions. She stood at the bar sipping wine, watching Jamal drift from one table to the next like a bee. Occasionally, he glanced her way or beckoned her to join him. She simply blew him a kiss. Without a notepad and a story idea, Kira found it difficult to interact with people she didn't know well. She had few friends and generally kept to herself. Putting on a show for a horny man was easier than being herself. She caught the eye of a young man who immediately stepped her way. The game was about to begin.

"You're Jamal's girlfriend, right?"

"Right." Kira eyed him, feigning great interest. He was shorter than she by maybe an inch, stocky with dark eyes, wavy black hair and a thick black moustache. Italian ancestry perhaps, or Greek, she guessed. Cute, but she would never disrespect her black brothers for a white man. She had decided that early on. While still in college she had gone to a nightclub with some classmates, both black and white. A young dark-haired man named Steve had asked her to dance. She accepted, thinking nothing of his white skin. He wore a sleeveless shirt and had muscular arms that Kira found attractive. For the rest of the night she hung out with him and his white friends — they cracked jokes and told stories that Kira found hysterical. As the evening wore on and the drinks continued to flow, everything was funny and she couldn't stop laughing. She was dancing with Steve, dancing close enough to brush against him, and they were both laughing. He pulled her closer and began rubbing his crotch against her hip. She giggled and swayed her hips to his rhythm.

"Yeah, that's my black bitch, lemme rub it on ya," he said, grinning.

Kira froze. She backed away from him, turned and walked out of the club. The moment confused her. Was it a tasteless faux pas, or had he believed she was his little black woman there to please him? She felt suspicious of white men after that — unsure of their underlying motives for being with a black woman. She often caught herself watching a mixed couple — black woman, white man — and wondering if, when they had sex, the man saw his woman as his black slave and himself as the master. (Perhaps the television series "Roots" had affected her young mind more than she had realized.) Kira looked at the man sitting next to her at the bar with satisfaction, knowing he wouldn't get the best of her.

"Jamal said you were something, and he was definitely right," the man said. His smile revealed a chipped front tooth that added to his charm. She blinked several times and pouted her painted lips, giving her best dumb girl impression, then thanked him for the compliment. She glanced at Jamal, who flashed her a smile while talking to a pretty blonde.

They played this game often at social events. She would flirt shamelessly with his friends or whoever came to her side, while Jamal watched her from a distance, pretending not to care until he couldn't stand it any longer and retrieved her for himself. It thrilled her to tease these pitiful men — usually white men she had no interest in — who were charmed by her and believed there was a glimmer of hope that she would sleep with them. It was all in the attitude. She didn't have to say much, just listen to them talk about themselves, laugh a lot and look longingly into their eyes while placing her fingers tenderly on her cleavage or her hips. Always their eyes followed her hands, sometimes deliberately, sometimes unconsciously. They would buy her drinks, despite her protests, and she would take only a few sips so that she didn't get drunk and lose control of the situation.

This man — his name was Gary — kept letting his eyes wander to her breasts, so she took deep breaths and sighed heavily, her chest rising and falling. She nodded frequently but heard little of what he said. He worked in accounting on the floor below Jamal's office; he thought Jamal was a great guy.

"I'm sure you are, too," she said.

Gary moved closer. "Wouldn't you like to find out?" His musk cologne stung her nostrils. Kira giggled, running her index finger around the rim of her wine glass and looking at him with sleepy eyes. This fool was moving much faster than most, perhaps hungry to be with a black woman, his head clouded by the sexual stereotype that black women were promiscuous. She searched for an acerbic let down.

"I got a room," he whispered, his head leaning closer to her face. "Jamal said y'all have an open relationship."

"What else did he say?" she asked.

Gary's warm beer breath smacked her cheek. "That you're hot in bed."

Amused, Kira sucked a drop of wine from the tip of her middle finger. Jamal had deliberately set up this poor soul. She blinked several times at him and covered her cleavage with her palm. "I can't believe he said that."

"I bet it's true."

She was tempted to give him a price, then decided it wasn't such a good idea for his co-workers to think Jamal was dating a hooker.

"Well, I do like it . . . a lot . . . but . . ." She licked her lips and sipped her drink. Casually, she searched the room for Jamal.

"I got protection." The man almost salivated on her shoulder.

"I don't think you'll need it for a hand job." She blew Gary a good-bye kiss and swayed provocatively across the room. Jamal caught her arm and swung her close to him, covering her mouth with his own. "Let's go upstairs," he whispered. Kira smiled. This part of the game she liked best. Jamal pinned her against the back of the elevator and kissed her mouth hard. They were barely inside the room when he was pushing her against the cold wall, kissing and licking her lips. Kira screamed and laughed as he tickled her. She fought him weakly, not wanting him to stop, enjoying the weight of his body covering her on the bed. She held on to him, clinging to the fantasy of forever until he rolled away, satisfied and ready to sleep. In no time, Jamal's snore sounded like a cat purring. Kira watched him for a moment, then turned her back to him and snuggled under the sheets, wrapping her arms around herself.

UNABLE TO sleep, she opened her eyes and looked into the dark hotel room. Sometimes, when the heat of sex had faded to a dull chill, she thought about old lovers, old moments that reawakened themselves for her mind to review and ask the same questions: Why? What would she do today? What could she have done differently? Did those old moments define who she was now? Paul's face assembled itself vividly in her mind, as if she had just seen him that day. Her first love. He'd had a long face with a long straight nose that made him look more Middle Eastern than of African descent, but his small wiry curls were a legacy from his Virginia mother. Kira had envied his unblemished mocha skin and his long eyelashes, and felt blessed every time he looked at her. She had seen him around the school but everybody knew he dated Denise, who was a senior, so any chance of a date with him was out of the question. They officially met at the first school dance of the year when she was in tenth grade and he was in eleventh grade. Kira was surprised to see him alone at the event, and dumbfounded when he asked her to dance to the Bee Gees' Saturday Night Fever. Paul struck a John Travolta pose, right hand raised, pointing to the ceiling, left hand on hip. Kira burst out laughing, as did he, and from that moment on it seemed all they did was laugh. She soon discovered that Denise had dumped him for a college freshman.

Kira and Paul dated for the rest of the year, spending many Saturday nights at the old drive-in movie theater, usually being chauffeured by Paul's cousin, a senior with a driver's license and a beat-up Camaro. Most often, they fogged up the car windows paying more attention to each other than the movie, while Paul's cousin stretched out with his girlfriend on a blanket covering the car's hood. Although Kira enjoyed the tingling along her inner thighs when their tongues touched, she grew nervous when Paul's fingers moved closer and closer to that most private part of her. Kira wasn't sure about having sex — after all, she was only fifteen — and steadfastly refused to "go all the way" until she felt absolutely certain she wanted it.

"Have you done it yet?" Beverly had asked one night on the phone.

"No!"

"What you waiting for?"

"I don't think I'm ready."

"I know I would be if I was dating Paul Washington. Girl, everyone knows he is the finest boy in town. Good-looking, athletic and smart. Hm, hm, hm."

The two of them burst into giggles. The notion of having sex with Paul kept Kira awake at night; it was obvious every time they were alone together that he wanted it. With all the fun they had at the movies, going to football games and hanging out at the ice-cream stand, Kira knew their relationship was about more than just sex. Still, she worried that he would lose interest if she kept saying no. On Paul's birthday, a month before school ended for the summer, Kira decided it was time. She took him home with her after school. Kenny was out playing with friends and her mother was working. In her twin bed, she gave Paul what he wanted. The sex hurt much more than expected, but she grew excited by Paul's grunts and moans in her ear as he pushed in and out of her; and when his entire body stiffened and shuddered, she knew she had made him happy. "That was awesome," he whispered. "Happy birthday," she said.

The next day, he didn't wait to eat lunch with her. Instead, he sat with a group of his friends, who snickered when she said hi to him. He kept his head down and wouldn't look at her. Kira stared at him, her cheeks beginning to burn as his friends smirked and hid their mouths behind their palms, whispering to each other. She turned and found a table on the other side of the cafeteria. When some girlfriends sat next to her, she couldn't speak to them, couldn't respond to their questions about why Paul sat elsewhere. Instinctively, they consoled her with hugs and comments. "He ain't worth it no-how," they said. After school, Kira locked herself in her room and sobbed into the pillow she had shared with Paul the afternoon before. For several days she couldn't eat, and whenever her brother came to see what was wrong, she screamed at him to get lost. She couldn't tell her mother what had happened. She couldn't tell anyone. "He doesn't love me anymore," was all Kira could say. Not that he had ever loved her, she knew this now. Love was an empty word. Dead air. Dust.

DR. DRE gave Kira a headache as he boomed through the speakers of Jamal's old sports car. Hard rap was too much for an early Sunday afternoon. She and Jamal had eaten brunch at the hotel and were heading back to her place to enjoy the rest of the day together. She already had dinner planned: steak with roasted potatoes and corn on the cob. Jamal's favorite. Kira didn't cook very often because it seemed like a waste of time just for herself, but she was excited to have someone over for a real dinner. Jamal pulled into the parking lot of her condominium complex, stopping behind Kira's jeep. He kept the engine running.

"I'll see you later," he said, leaning toward her for a kiss.

"You're not coming in?"

"Nah, I got some stuff to do." He angled the rear-view mirror to look at himself, bared his teeth as if checking for pieces of food, and then flipped the mirror back into place.

"What kind of stuff?"

"Just stuff, Kira. Nothing to concern your pretty self about. I'll call you later."

"I bought steaks for dinner."

"Another night, okay?" His foot pumped the gas pedal.

Always, when she began to think maybe their relationship

could be about more than just sex, he turned into a patronizing asshole and she remembered that she didn't want to spend the rest of her life with him. Their relationship was *not* a forever love. They played games, that was all. She wouldn't be vulnerable, wouldn't let her guard down and reveal that deep inside she was like every other girl — she just wanted a man to love her.

Kira kissed him lightly on the lips, slid out of the vehicle and slammed the door so hard that the car rocked. Jamal winced, and she grinned.

12

A LITTLE before noon, Kira strolled down the hallway from the Features department into the newsroom where she found Beverly yelling across the expanse to an editor that someone was on hold for him. Beverly rolled her eyes and snorted, then announced, "If anyone needs me, I've gone to lunch." She had one of those low sexy voices that Kira could muster only when she had a cold. In high school, Beverly sang bass in the choir. Now, as the newspaper's editorial assistant, she barked announcements through the newsroom. "Girl, sometimes I wonder," she said. "What am I doing at this newspaper?"

Kira smiled. She knew exactly what Beverly meant.

The Minority Affairs Committee meeting was scheduled for twelve-fifteen at the downtown deli. The pair walked on the shaded side of Main Street, a warm breeze guiding them along. They had known each other since childhood, having both grown up on Richmond Avenue in the center of Fort Lewis' black neighborhood. Although Beverly's parents had moved out to the suburbs just when the girls were preparing to enter high school, Beverly persuaded her folks to let her attend North High with Kira. Back then, Kira had trusted Beverly to keep her secrets, like the time she skipped a day in middle school to see a movie with Jackson Smith. While Beverly had lamented that no boys were asking *her* out to the movies, she wrote the note anyway, nervously forging Kira's mother's name.

Back then the two girls were inseparable; they called each other sisters — but not anymore. They didn't share secrets anymore, didn't talk about the men in their lives. They kept their conversations focused on jobs and family.

Back then, they had both applied and been accepted to the journalism program at Virginia State, but in their sophomore year Beverly had gotten pregnant and dropped out. The father had been a junior and encouraged her to get rid of the baby, but Beverly refused, going home to raise the child herself. Kira had admired her decision although wasn't so sure she would have done the same if she had been in her friend's shoes. Kira didn't believe she herself had the strength and patience needed to raise a child alone, but she stuck by her friend and helped care for the baby girl, named Tamika, whenever she was home during breaks. When Beverly asked her to be Tamika's godmother, Kira cried with joy.

As the years progressed, Kira became more promiscuous and Beverly clung to each man who showed her any interest.

Tony Brown had grown up on Richmond Avenue with Kira and Beverly. He was older by a few years, and Kira had never liked him much then. He always acted like he knew everything. He had lived with his grandmother, didn't make it through high school, and hung out with petty hustlers trying to be some big time gangster. After a few arrests, he finally got several years for grand larceny. Beverly had run into him one evening at the 7-11. He had told her he would need a place to stay once the parole officer said he could leave the halfway house.

Kira didn't know much about their relationship or how he had sweet-talked his way into Beverly's life, and her apartment. She had dropped in to visit Beverly one Saturday afternoon. Tamika was at her grandmother's. Tony sat on the couch, said hello and quickly disappeared into the bedroom where he stayed for much of the visit. When he reappeared, he silently slithered through the room and stepped out onto the balcony to smoke. "Is it getting serious?" Kira asked. Beverly shrugged. Tony stepped back into the room and told Beverly they had to leave soon. He had a hair appointment and needed her to drive him there because he didn't have a car of his own. The fact that he didn't have a job, either, didn't come up. He neither made eye contact nor spoke a word to Kira. What did her friend see in him? From what Kira could tell, he had nothing in common with Beverly, who was passionate about many things, loved life, loved to laugh, loved new experiences. Kira considered Beverly her sister and wanted to protect her; she did *not* want to see her sister get hurt again by some loser boyfriend. (Beverly's last boyfriend had been dating three other women at the same time and telling each one she was his only love.) The potential loomed large for this one to use her up, drain her money and dump her.

As Beverly locked the front door and Tony went on ahead to the car, Kira told her she could do better. "Don't sell yourself short," she said.

"He makes me laugh," said Beverly. "Besides, it's better than being by myself."

From that moment on, Beverly shared nothing with Kira about him. Although Kira didn't like him, she would have been open to seeing him through her friend's eyes, hearing about what he did that made her love him so. Instead, their conversations shrank, and Kira kept her opinions and questions to herself. Kira never mentioned him again. She never mentioned how hurt she was that Beverly valued him far above Kira despite their years of friendship, that suddenly Kira couldn't express her opinion or disagree with Beverly and continue to be her friend. Beverly cut her off. And Kira let her. Even after Tony found someone new and walked out on Beverly, they never talked about it.

So they strolled to the deli commenting on the warm weather, on the politics of the newsroom, and Kira said nothing about wishing they were sisters again. She said nothing about her father.

PETE AND Patricia sat at a small table in the back of the cramped seating area. Kira and Beverly stood in line for food then nudged their way through to join them. The four made up the only non-white section of the news department, which included sports and features. The black sports reporter had left six months ago, and

The New York Times had snapped up the other black news reporter months before that. Beverly had joined the paper as newsroom assistant a year before Kira, and had in fact given Kira a heads up about the opening for a general reporter's position. Since then, from what Kira could tell, no effort had been made to hire more black reporters or editors despite the city's population being almost thirty-percent black, ten-percent Asian and two-percent Hispanic.

Cate and David arrived just as the four had settled into their seats. The two arrivals were the only non-black staffers who had expressed any interest or encouragement when Beverly formed the committee a year ago to address concerns that the newspaper was not covering non-white communities. With some white participation, Beverly quickly got management's blessing and the group began meeting every month, but over the past year, the newspaper had yet to reflect the city's growing diversity.

With everyone now at the table, Beverly pulled out a copy of the article that prompted the impromptu meeting with sections highlighted in yellow. "Some of these quotes are unnecessary. This one resident says, 'These black boys don't even live here and come in and steal from us.' Now, please don't tell me it's only black people who are stealing from these neighborhoods?"

"From what I understand, there has been a rise in break-ins in the neighborhood and one of the arrests made was an African American teenager," said Cate.

"I'm not saying blacks don't steal shit, but don't tell me there are no white kids stealing," said Beverly. "Why focus on this one predominantly white neighborhood? Why not look at the city as a whole and get more statistics on overall crime?"

"This is part of a series, I think," Cate said.

Beverly stared at her. "Whose side are you on?"

Deep lines mapped Cate's creamy face, charting the years she had worked as a journalist in various cities across the country. She was a senior reporter at *The Fort Lewis Times* with a sharp eye for creating stories that cut to the heart of the issue. "It's not about being on any particular side," she said. "I'm just trying to be fair."

"Well, it's insulting," Pete said. "And it's obvious to me this piece has got nothing to do with being fair."

What was fair anymore, Kira wondered. A few months ago, the newspaper had printed pictures of young black men arrested on drug charges and left out their white cohorts. Having a diversity committee in place might make management look good, but real change would come years and years from now. The chatter swirled in circles. Tired of the conversation, of the struggle to balance the news coverage, Kira contributed little. She remembered seeing Pete's name assigned to the Native American festival tomorrow. By far the best photographer on the staff, Pete was reliable and always produced quality pictures that matched Kira's stories perfectly. She conceded that maybe she was biased because he was black, but she did feel more comfortable with him. She could relate to him in a way she couldn't relate to his white counterparts. This connection was subtle. A cultural bond that expressed itself through words and rhythms the non-black community didn't fully understand. Besides, he was from Philadelphia and didn't think small the way most folks did around Fort Lewis.

The group decided to present a formal statement of displeasure to the managing editor at the reporter's meeting on Monday with the intention of creating some discussion around the issue of race. She hoped this could be a turning point for change.

13

SHE AWOKE suddenly out of a vivid dream that faded as soon as her eyes opened. When she realized the day and time, she began to panic. Richard Harper had invited her to a sunrise ceremony not open to the public, and Kira knew she was late before looking at the clock.

The sky was slate gray as she sped down the highway. She opened the windows to let cool air swirl around her head. Trees and homes appeared as looming shadows along the way. As she approached the field where the event was to take place, she could see a fire blazing in the distance. She parked at the community center and walked across the knobbly grass toward the group of people dancing around the fire. Smoke rippled into the sky, now brightening with the sun, the air tangy in her nostrils. A large man stopped her as she approached, telling her this was a private event and the powwow would open at nine. Kira explained that she was a newspaper reporter and that Richard Harper had invited her. The man seemed suspicious but took her to where Richard was sitting. He stood up and welcomed her with a firm handshake. He introduced her to the people seated around him, tribal leaders from across the country here to offer their support and enjoy the festivities. They sat in fold-up chairs near the fire, which burned in a shallow pit in the ground and was built up at least three or four feet high. Near them were five men pounding on one large drum. Men and women moved clockwise around the fire, bobbing slightly and tapping their feet with each step to the beat of the drums.

Some of the women wore shells around their ankles to give melody to the music. She asked why the event was not open to the public.

"This is the Stomp Dance. It's a sacred dance of the Cherokee people to honor the Great Spirit," Richard said. "It's part of our tradition, not something we share with the public. The powwow today is to raise funds and awareness. It caters to the non-Indians, and we lay it on thick with the souvenirs. What you see there is only partly representative of our traditions. But this, this is part of our spiritual heritage. It's not for sale." He smiled and Kira nodded, honored to be a witness to the private ceremony.

Richard's parents, Elaine and Big Bear, danced in the circle side by side. Farther back, she saw Alex wearing a brown smock with colorful ribbons attached to it. Kira watched the group moving gracefully, methodically, around the fire's ragged glow, their faces content. She leaned back in the chair and relaxed.

AS THE powwow got under way, the lush valley soaked in the sun's heat, which was reflected in the ruddy faces crowding the event. People packed the field. Drums, chimes and laughter filled the air, energizing Kira as she made her way toward the huge picnic tent shading most of the booths. Kira wandered from one booth to the next, talking to people while eyeing the intricate beadwork, the silver jewelry, the t-shirts and traditional Native American dresses. Vendors had come from as far away as New Mexico and Arizona. One Choctaw woman from Oklahoma said she traveled almost all year round selling her jewelry at festivals and conferences. She, like many, was donating fifty percent of her profits to help with the purchase of the land. "It's about unity. Helping our people," she said.

Big Bear's booth stood in the center of the excitement, the man himself fanning his face with a cluster of feathers. Elaine sat next to him sewing ribbons on burnt orange smocks.

"Ah, the reporter," Elaine said, rising from her metal chair. "Welcome." She wrapped her arms firmly around Kira, engulfing her. The embrace felt warm and safe, and Kira could have held on forever; something in the hug triggered emotions Kira wasn't sure she could control. In the last few days, emotions had flooded her: confusion, uncertainty, a sudden desire to seek out this man who was her father, to find out what made her who she was, to understand her identity. The Harper family held something special in its knowledge of itself, something that seemed out of Kira's grasp. She pulled away, suppressing the sensations with a laugh. Big Bear raised his fan to his forehead as if to salute her.

"In that story you're writing, make sure you spell our names right," Elaine said. Her face crinkled into a smile. "If you want my Indian name, it's Kicking Crow."

"Why don't you use your Indian names all the time?"

"Some do. Some don't. In this society, it's just easier to use Anglo names," said Elaine said. "Do you see anything you like?"

Kira had seen plenty of things she liked. Blue velvet covered the large table where statues and trinkets from the shop had been carefully placed. A jewelry case sat at one end of the table and in it she spotted the wolf pendant Alex had tried to sell to her.

"It's beautiful, ain't it," Elaine said, as if she had read Kira's thoughts. "One of a kind. My grandson's got quite a knack with silver."

"It is extraordinary."

Kira headed toward the performance area, marked off with bales of hay that doubled as seating. The steady drumbeats and singing were invigorating as she meandered through the festivities. The aroma of sweet berries and buffalo burgers on a grill made her stomach rumble. She spotted Pete focusing his lens at an elderly Native American woman settling herself on a hay bale. Kira moved toward him, but a body rushing past caused her to lose sight of the photographer. The throbbing drum stopped and Kira heard the announcer welcoming everyone to the event. She made her way to the dancing area and peeked through a crowd forming around the perimeter. When she heard Alex's name, she stood on her tiptoes to get a better view. As the drums began again, pounding a constant rhythm, she saw a man wearing only tan leather pants and moccasins standing at the far end of the circle. Alex. Feathers shimmered around his head as he moved, some fluttering upwards and others falling flat against his forehead and cheeks to blend with the black and white lines painted on his skin. His body quivered, glistening with the heat from the sun. He moved slowly around the open space. He bent low, arms outstretched, and then raised himself up only to swoop low again. In an instant, he was bouncing rhythmically across the open space, his knees bobbing pony-like as he stamped his feet. The drumming vibrated in Kira's chest.

"It's the dance of the hawk," a voice whispered in her ear. Richard Harper stood behind her, his feathered headdress more magnificent than the one worn by his son. "He dances to honor the bird's spirit. The hawk is sacred to our clan. It's a symbol of strength and courage."

Mesmerized by Alex, she watched the muscles in his arms, his chest and his thighs as he swayed and pounded to the beat. She saw the concentration in his eyes and wanted to be there with him wherever his mind was. She imagined herself joining in the dance, freeing her spirit to shake and spin and chant, but knew she would never do it. If this were an African celebration, would she feel more comfortable dancing a traditional dance in front of an audience? Not likely. Kira was an observer. She stood back and viewed the world from a distance, taking notes and telling other people's stories, silently choosing her angle and manipulating it to her advantage. She didn't plunge into anything without weighing the pros and cons and making a calculated decision.

Yet, watching Alex made her want to shake loose and connect with something that would give her a sense of belonging. Kira had never before ventured to any of the Native American festivals she had seen advertised. The drums, the dancing and elaborate garments enthralled her. She liked the warmth that oozed from the Indian people, liked their rituals and respect for the earth.

The drums stopped, and Richard excused himself, pushing his way into the ring to introduce a new group of Native dancers from Oklahoma. Alex drifted away into the crowd on the other side. Kira moved through the throng of people searching for him. Someone pulled at her ear and she turned quickly. Alex stood before her, breathless and grinning, now wearing a loose-fitting shirt. Words caught in her throat. Her palms were damp, and she fought a desire to run away from him. She looked down, pretending to study her notes.

"So, tell me about this dance of the hawk?" she asked, allowing herself only a quick glance at him.

"My uncle taught me. He's really a close friend of my father's, but I call him uncle. His uncle had taught him."

"A family tradition?"

Alex nodded. He watched her intently.

"Your father said you dance to respect the bird."

"It's said that when our ancestors Quiet Hawk and Long Arrow died in battle, the hawk came down from the sky and carried them both to the Spirit World."

Kira studied his face as he talked. His straight nose, his high cheekbones, and his light brown skin reminded her of smooth caramel. She looked at the feathered headdress framing his face. Hawk feathers. He nodded and fingered them carefully. "They were handed down through the generations."

So much tradition. "I can't imagine having sacred things that belonged to my ancestors," she said. "I never even met my paternal grandparents and my mother's parents both died when I was young." She thought for a moment about her father, and her grandparents. For a moment she pictured an old white couple, then shook the image away. "It must mean a lot to have them."

Alex smiled and nodded again. He was looking at her the way men did before they asked her to dance, before they bought her a drink or invited her home. She shifted her weight from one hip to the other, and had they been in a bar, she would have slipped easily into that familiar role. In this setting and with this man, however, that role was out of place. She enjoyed his attention, yet instead of feeling sexy and confident, his scrutiny panicked her. He asked if she had any more questions. Her words escaped her in a whisper. "What do you think about when you dance?"

"Nothing, nothing at all."

The air around them expanded and all noise and activity fell away leaving them cocooned in a moment of possibility. Until a voice, like a brick falling into a pond, startled them back to reality. A young woman grabbed Alex's arm, kissed his cheek and showered him with praise. Kira gaped at the woman, his fiancée, recognizing her from the photograph in Alex's apartment. Much shorter than Alex, Lorett stood only as high as his chest. Her suede dress hugged her slim hips, fringes dancing around her knees as she moved. Lorett tugged at his sleeve. People wanted to meet him, she said. "They're interested in your work. Come on," she insisted.

Alex gave Kira a look as if to apologize and Lorett seemed to notice Kira for the first time. He introduced the two women and Lorett asked if she had interrupted an interview. Kira took a small step backwards and said she would finish the interview later. She watched the woman lead him away through the crowd. He looked back at Kira as he put his arm around Lorett's shoulders. Kira stared at the brown earth beneath her feet, then drifted away in search of Pete, who was zooming in on an array of colorful beads at one of the vendors' tables. They chatted for a moment, and once she made sure he had gotten pictures of Alex's dance, she left for the office to write the story. Because it was Saturday and the newsroom wouldn't fill up until later in the day, no one would disturb her. Words flowed almost unconsciously from her fingertips, words describing the brown earth and the many who had staked claim to it, and those who wanted to reclaim it once again as theirs.

CLOUDS SWIRLED, alternately hiding and revealing the half moon. Kira pressed the buzzer and waited for Jamal to let her in. Nothing sheltered her from the cool wind breezing past the door of his apartment building. It was after nine and she wanted him to be home. While this wouldn't be the first time she had shown up unexpectedly to find him out, Kira didn't make a habit of arriving at his door unannounced. She pushed the button again, waited a moment. As she turned to leave, his voice came quietly through the speaker. She shouted her name, not meaning to sound so excited by his response, and the door clicked open. Kira felt weepy and wanted to lose herself in his embraces, but she had to play it cool or else turn him off. Jamal didn't like needy women. Most often she maintained the persona of a strong black woman who didn't need anybody, but there were days she simply wanted to curl up in someone's arms and have him make the world go away. Like now, when she was feeling unsettled, envious. What would it be like to know your family line hundreds of years back, to have a future already paved with certainty? Her future was vague enough, and now she wasn't sure of the past she thought she had known. She wanted to bury her head under the covers and forget about Larry Walsh. Forget he was suddenly alive, and that he was white. Forget her mother had been lying about him for all these years. Forget everything.

She let her clothes fall at the bedside and climbed on top of Jamal, straddling his waist. She held his hands, moving them across her skin and pulling them away when he reached for her nipples. Then she locked his hands with hers on the pillow above his head and kissed his mouth aggressively, biting his lower lip and rocking her hips back and forth. His guttural moans excited her and she pushed harder until his body tensed in silence.

She imagined Alex there beneath her, his long hair spread across the pillow.

14

*T*HERE ARE *many stories my grandmother used to tell. Stories that place us on the land we're trying to get back. Let me tell you this particular story you may find interesting. Many years ago, sometime after the Revolutionary War, a slave girl was taken in by my people. Often the Indian people harbored runaway slaves. The story goes that she escaped with her family from South Carolina, but her mother and brother died as they journeyed north. The Cherokees named her Braided Hair on account of her hairstyle. She wore cornrows like the African people do. She lived with the Cherokee and took on our ways and fell in love with one of our warriors, Eagle Wing. Women considered him one of the most handsome men in all the clans. Much to the sadness of many girls, Eagle Wing took Braided Hair as his wife. He was an Indian warrior through my grandmother's ancestral line. He was killed, though, in a fierce battle. Braided Hair had no child to care for. She was so distraught by the death of her husband that she plunged a knife into her heart and fell into Deer Creek. Her blood flowed into the wading pools where the wapato grew, killing the plant forever. The wapato has never bloomed since. It's said that her soul wanders the Earth and his wanders the Heavens in search of each other. When they reunite, the wapato will bloom and flourish in Deer Creek as it once did.*

15

HER MOTHER had called twice, leaving messages on her home phone and at the newspaper asking if she was okay. But Kira wasn't ready to talk to her mother. Not yet. Her mother's revelation about Larry Walsh had only deepened Kira's confusion about who she was and who she thought she should be, between what she wanted and what she had.

At Christmastime she had experienced a longing to understand her purpose in life. Instead of being buoyed by the holiday spirit, its weight pinned her down. Usually, she began marking off on the calendar (starting a week before Thanksgiving) the number of days until Santa was to bring her gifts; her presents for others already bought and hidden away. This time, the holiday season had crept upon her and at the last possible moment she had dragged herself to the shopping malls to become Santa Claus for each person on her gift list. Suddenly, she hated the frenetic experience. Hoping it would raise her spirits, she had decided to celebrate Kwanzaa but couldn't find a Kinara, which didn't come as a surprise. Fort Lewis was what she called a small-town city — too many residents for it to be a small town, but too many small-minded people for it to be a city. Nestled in a valley between the Allegheny and Blue Ridge mountains, its tallest building reached all of sixteen floors. The wealthy lived in pretty brick houses near downtown or in spacious cookie-cutter boxes out in the suburbs. They liked to talk of themselves as down-home folks, then boast of their shopping trips to New York and vacations in the Caymans.

The poor blacks lived in rundown neighborhoods to the west of downtown while the poor whites lived in trailer parks on the east-side. To the average resident, a Kinara could just as easily have been an exotic bird from the islands. Not to be dissuaded, however, Kira decided to make her own and bought seven brass candleholders. Green and red candles were easy to find, but she had no luck finding any black ones. To her surprise, she did find a slim soft-cover book on Kwanzaa, which she read in line at the checkout counter. The celebration, she thought, would give her some grounding, add a sense of belonging and cultural unity, a moment to reflect on African-American heritage.

On Christmas Eve, she hadn't known where Jamal was. She sat on her living room floor wrapping gifts — silk briefs and Armani cologne for Jamal; a pink nightgown and matching robe for her mother; casual shirts and socks for her brother; a coffee-table book on locomotives for Uncle Buster; a couple of hardback mysteries for Aunt Mae; bubble bath and perfume for Beverly; and a dress for Beverly's daughter, Tamika. The gifts weren't especially creative, but at least she had something for everybody. She thought about calling her mother but knew she would be at church. She didn't want to be alone, yet didn't quite know who she wanted by her side, didn't quite know what was missing.

She woke early on Christmas morning and lay under the covers feeling like a bag of coal. As a child, she remembered waking with her brother before sunrise and tumbling down the wooden stairs to the fake shimmering Christmas tree that seemed a hundred feet tall. Every year, each branch, covered with tiny silver spikes instead of pine needles, had to be inserted into a wooden pole, and like magic, the box of bits and pieces became a grand shining vision of Christmas. If she remembered correctly, her stepfather, Daddy J, had brought it home when she was seven. Beneath the tree sat boxes covered in Santa and reindeer wrapping paper and filled with new winter clothes, a Barbie doll for Kira, and a GI Joe for Kenny. And there were always tangerines. She never knew why, but figured Santa wanted her and her brother to be healthy. She remembered the year she got her first bike, red with thick white tires. But her memories were running together; that was before Kenny, and before the silver tree. That was when Kira and her mother lived in an upstairs apartment, just the two of them.

She showered and dressed and arrived at her mother's house just after ten to help prepare dinner.

"What time did you say Kenny was getting here?" Martha asked, shoving the stuffing into the turkey. Sweat glistened on her forehead and cheeks from the warm kitchen.

Kira sat at the table grating cheese for the macaroni. "He didn't call you?"

"No, he didn't call me." Martha opened the oven door and placed the pan containing the twelve-pound bird in the oven. "You said he was gonna be late."

"I dunno Ma. You know your son as well as I do. He'll get here when he gets here." Kira pinched some grated cheese and dropped it in her mouth. "When's Mae and Buster coming?"

"Supposed to be here at noon," Martha said. "But I guess around two by the time Mae figures out what she wants to wear."

Martha chuckled and Kira responded with a half-hearted grin. She watched her mother wash and rinse dishes in the sink. She was two shades darker and several sizes bigger than Kira. She had lost her svelte figure in her thirties after giving birth to Kenny, and although she often wished to be a size six again, Martha said she accepted her size would fluctuate between sixteen and eighteen. Kira didn't want to grow old, have her body expand and be alone for the rest of her life like her mother. Ma's life seemed like such a dismal existence — although as Kira considered her own life, there wasn't much to rave about there.

"You do realize this is Christmas dinner we're preparing and not a funeral wake?" her mother said, wiping her hands on a linen towel. Kira said she was tired and hadn't slept well. Martha pulled a wooden chair out from the table and sat down. "What's the matter?" Kira shook her head. Just tired.

"I remember when you would get so excited on Christmas Eve, you'd want to stay awake to catch a glimpse of Santa Claus," her mother said. "But then I'd find you snoring with your raggedy puppy dog in your arms. You weren't trying to stay up for Santa this time, were you?"

Kira kept her focus on the cheese as it fell in clumps on the plate. "Yeah, Ma. That was it. Up waiting for Santa."

"You can cut out the sarcasm."

She stopped grating, looked at her mother and shrugged. "It doesn't feel like Christmas anymore. It's all about spending money and women slaving over stoves and sinks while men do whatever they want. It's not about love and family."

Martha smiled. "Sure it is. Food holds us together, sweetheart. This here is a time for family to gather and share fellowship, to celebrate the Lord's birthday and what He's done for us." She poked the table with her forefinger. "That's what Christmas is all about. You should have come with me to the evening service last night. That would have lifted your spirits." She rose from her seat and looked at her daughter. "Your problem is, you refuse to open your heart to the Lord."

Kira sighed. Her mother's answer to everything was Jesus Christ. "I'm a heathen, Ma, you know that."

"So you keep telling me, but even a heathen can be saved."

Aunt Mae and Uncle Buster arrived a little after three. Martha gave Kira a knowing wink to acknowledge it was well beyond the scheduled time. Mae was older than Martha by three years — flashier in style with big African-style earrings, a closely-cropped silver Afro and a red chenille sweater. Buster was Mae's third husband. Aunt Mae's bubbly aura helped lift Kira's mood. Before sitting to eat, they stood around the dining table and joined hands. Martha thanked God for bringing her family together and asked for her son's safe journey from Washington, D.C. She asked that He continue to bless them with good health and warm hearts. Kira gripped her mother's hot hand on her right and felt the thick hand of Uncle Buster in her left. She took a deep breath and said her own short, silent prayer. "God, help me find my way."

KENNY FINALLY arrived a little after five o'clock to a hug and a swat on the ear from his mother for being so late. But he made up for it with silk blouses and earrings for both his mother and sister. He even had a bottle of bourbon for his uncle and perfume for his aunt. Kira was impressed. While their mother and aunt chatted in the kitchen, and Uncle Buster started to snore on the couch, Kira and Kenny escaped to his room where she quizzed him on this fabulous Christmas Eve party that had ended sometime around five in the morning. He stretched out on his single bed in the room he had grown up in. She settled on the floor and raked through his music. They talked about the party, and Kira asked if anyone famous showed up; if they had, Kenny said, he hadn't seen them. She asked him about school and he told her he was considering graduate school. His drive to succeed both amazed her and made her proud of him. He was studying philosophy with a minor in English at American University and scheduled to graduate in the fall. A full scholarship and a part-time job in a bar helped pay his way. He rarely came home, calling when he needed money. And Ma wired cash every time. Kira figured her mother responded, to some extent, out of guilt. His father had been barely a shadow in their lives. In a way, Kira felt bad for him too, knowing the misery of seeing fathers showing up at basketball games to cheer on their youngsters — Kenny's classmates.

Of course, Kira had endured a similar fate. She had sung in the school choir and had danced in her high school's version of "Guys & Dolls," only to be whisked home afterward with a neighbor because her mother had to work late.

Each knew they had different fathers. Kira had believed hers to be long dead to a foreign war before she could speak. But for a short while Kenny's father had been her daddy, too. She remembered him wrapping his large hands around her waist and throwing her in the air above his head, then catching her safely and snuggling her into his chest. She remembered laughing a lot when he came around, always tickling or chasing or teasing her. She couldn't remember another time when her mother had laughed so much, as well. Kira had liked it when just the three of them were together, but recalled her joy when Kenny was born because it meant she would be part of a real family with a brother and a daddy. Daddy J she called him, since he wasn't her real father. She liked having a daddy. Then one day he was there, and the next, Daddy J was gone. Kenny had been around two or three. Kira was afraid to ask what happened, hoping that one day he would simply show up again. Kenny, on the other hand, had asked repeatedly, "When's Daddy coming back? Where did he go?" His baby mouth barely able to form the words. Ma never gave a straight answer. "He's just gone," she said.

In the months that followed, Kenny often woke up yelling at his father. One night, Kira found him crouched on the floor by his bed, on his side of the room, stabbing a teddy bear with scissors. She was afraid to approach him, but his chest heaved so heavily from crying that she swooped in to wrap him in her arms and comfort him. Finally, he let the scissors drop from his small hand, and she held him tightly for a long time while he wept. Even though Daddy J had meant as much to Kira as he had to Kenny, she could soothe herself with the fact that he wasn't her real daddy. It was easier to say your father was dead than that he had disappeared.

"I can't imagine you teaching English," she said, still imagining Kenny as a little boy playing with action figures.

"And why not? I have a grand command of the English language," he said, attempting a British accent. He laughed as Kira cut her eyes at him. "How's things at the newspaper? You still in the features department?"

"Yeah, still there, dealing with the same old crap. Still no more blacks in management despite our little committee, and the same old crony reporters keep getting their names on the front page with the same old so-called investigative stories." Kira sighed. "I'm thinking of leaving. I could get a lot more money in public relations."

"I thought you loved journalism."

She did love journalism. She loved telling people's stories, discovering gems in the community and sharing their charm with everyone else. Playing with words to get the story just right. But the last few years the editors had shown less and less interest in the language, in good writing, and spent most of the time cutting words to make room for advertisements. She could spend several days interviewing and writing a strong story that ultimately got dumped right before publication or landed on the back page. Would it be any better at another newspaper?

"Would you move outta town?" Kenny asked.

"If it wasn't for Ma, I'd have moved years ago."

"She'll beg you to stay."

"I know, but I'm almost thirty, Kenny. I've got to get a new life with some excitement, and that won't happen around here. You got out. Why can't I?"

"Mothers always want their daughters by their sides. Besides, it was your decision to leave Charlotte and come back to Fort Lewis."

Ma hadn't asked her outright to come back; her request had been unspoken. Kira dutifully packed up her new life at the *Charlotte Observer* to come home and sit by her mother's side while she recovered from the heart attack.

"What about you and whatsisname, Jamie?"

"It's Jamal," Kira said, still annoyed at her brother.

She and Jamal had been together about a year and a half but marriage and children were not in their future. Kenny asked if she wanted to get married. She thought for a moment. The answer seemed complicated. Yes, she wanted marriage, wanted to exchange vows of forever and snuggle against a warm body every night. Yet the thought of getting married and settling down in a town that kept looking backward instead of into the future was not what she wanted. She couldn't see a future, a life filled with wonder and options and ideas. Fort Lewis offered nothing but the same forevermore. She leaned against the wall and looked around her baby brother's room. A poster of a frowning Janet Jackson during her "Control" phase remained taped to the wall alongside magazine cutouts of Jordan and Magic. These days, she and Kenny were closer, now that they had grown up. In those early years, Kenny had constantly gotten on her nerves. Because of the six years between them, she had to be the responsible one assigned to watch him every night while their mother worked the evening shift at the hospital. Instead of being free to do what she wanted, Kira had been stuck with her annoying know-it-all little brother.

While he could still be a smart-ass, he had grown into a warm and gentle young man. Something about Kenny's expression made her think of Daddy J. Did her brother look like him? She couldn't clearly remember the man's face, just a faded image of his smile, his big hands and his deep laugh. She wondered why he had left. Had it been the responsibility of two kids that had scared him away, or had he simply stopped loving her mother? After two heartaches, no wonder Ma never settled down with anyone.

The itch to seek out something new in her life had stayed with Kira as the January snowstorms masked the hills and valleys of Southwest Virginia. She trudged to work to write stories about how the weather was affecting the city. She and Pete, the photographer, slid around town trying to find "extraordinary people doing amazing things" as her editor had put it. She wrote a lengthy story on how adversity brings communities together, citing the Truckers Association helping the elderly get to the grocery stores and a group of unorganized teens who dug out driveways, babysat and ran errands in their neighborhood. For some the spirit of Christmas had struck all over again, or perhaps in some cases, for the first time. But the candles on the Kinara that Kira had bought on Christmas Eve remained unlit.

As the winter continued, Kira helped her mother get around town in the four-wheel drive Jeep that Jamal had insisted she buy. While she had been somewhat skeptical about getting the truck, in a snowstorm it didn't seem like such an extravagance. One day, while pulling groceries from the back seat, she had suggested that her mother get a vehicle with four-wheel drive.

"Child, don't be ridiculous. I can't afford something like this."

"Not like this. There're some nice cars you can get. Thompson's Used Cars often has good deals."

"I got you to help me, don't I?" her mother said.

The conversation turned to her brother, who had called their mother a week or so ago to check in and ask for money. Typical. He had asked how Kira was doing with her job search. One of the plastic bags slipped from Kira's gloved hand. She hadn't told her mother about her desire to apply for a job out of state, although her applications to the *Washington Post* and the *Atlanta Journal and Constitution* had been sitting on her kitchen table for over a week now. Kira looked at her mother and was surprised to see her face bright and smiling.

"I really shouldn't expect you to stay here just for me."

"Let's get inside where we can talk," Kira suggested. "It's cold out here."

They tidied away the groceries, and Martha put the kettle on for tea.

Kira sat at the kitchen table trying to soften her eagerness to get away from Fort Lewis. "I could switch to public relations. I might find a position like that around here." She knew she wasn't interested in a public relations career but the words tumbled out of her from the guilt she felt at leaving her mother.

"You don't have to stay on account of me. I'd be a fool to think you'd want to live here the rest of your life without seeing something of the world."

Kira was relieved. "It's not you," she said to make her mother feel better.

"That's good to know." Her mother's smile widened.

"I just need more than life is giving me here. More of a challenge, maybe. A bigger paper in a bigger city would give me that, I guess."

Her mother asked about Jamal, but Kira assured her their relationship was not serious.

"He's such a nice young man. And doing well for himself. What is it he does again? Marketing?"

"He's the assistant director of sales, Ma. He is good at what he does, but I don't think he's the marrying kind. He still wants to sow his oats. And besides, I'm not ready for marriage either."

Her mother nodded, yet she looked sad, and instantly Kira felt another rush of guilt and frustration. Except for the four years in college and the six-month internship at the paper in North Carolina, Fort Lewis was all she knew. The *Fort Lewis Times* had an opening for a junior reporter, and she got the job covering the cops and courts beat. She lived with her mother for as long as she could stand it, then moved into a dingy downtown apartment until she had saved enough for a down payment on a condo in the suburbs. Far enough away to feel independent, but close enough to be at her mother's side in a hurry. These days, the urge to bolt from Fort Lewis and stop only when her muscles and breath couldn't carry her any farther was overwhelming. She had grown tired of dunking her boredom in wine and playing games with Jamal to appease her loneliness. A new city offered the chance to recreate herself into someone brave and confident. To discard the past and begin anew.

16

WITH THE warmer weather, business started to pick up at Big Bear's Cabin — spring brought tourists. Alex hated managing the shop's day-to-day business, especially the bookkeeping with the old ledger, pencil in hand, subtracting the bills he had paid that day and tallying the sales receipts — it took forever. A computer would make his life much easier, and he was determined to get one and bring the store into the modern world. After all, in only a few years, the twentieth century would draw to a close.

He stepped outside the shop, taking a break from the paperwork and leaned on the window ledge beside his grandfather, who sat in his usual place at the door.

"What do you say to us getting a computer, PawPaw?"

Big Bear raised an eyebrow at his grandson. "What are you talking about?"

"A computer. You know what a computer is, don't you?"

"I know what a computer is." He chipped away at a thick twig in his hand. "What you going to do with a computer?"

"Keep our accounts balanced for one thing."

"Machines are only as good as the hand that cranks them."

Alex figured he wouldn't win this conversation and kept silent. The air blew fresh and he inhaled deeply. Ms. Wilson, his old high-school math teacher, strolled along with her terrier on the other side of the street. When she waved, he raised his arm in response. Instantly, she headed toward him and he heard his grandfather groan.

"Now you done it. Here she comes," Big Bear grumbled.

Amused, Alex patted his grandfather on the shoulder. "She won't bite you, I don't think."

For years, Ms. Wilson had made it clear she adored his grandfather, who had never grown comfortable with her flirtations.

"Well, Alex Harper, it sure is good to see you around town," she said, as she approached. "We all missed you for sure." She adjusted her chiffon scarf around her neck and tugged the leash as her dog strained to reach the lamppost a few feet away. Ms. Wilson had mellowed considerably in her retirement and had lost the perpetual frown she had worn in those years teaching high school. Alex thanked her for her kind words. "It's good to be back."

He took a step toward the store's entrance.

"And how are you, Mr. Harper? Looking sharp as always."

Big Bear nodded but kept focused on his work and didn't see the smile she flashed him.

"So when's the big day?" she asked Alex. "You set a date yet, or am I not supposed to know nothing about it?"

As far as he could tell the entire town knew about the engagement and impending wedding the day after he proposed. "There's nothing set yet. Likely, next spring."

"Well, you couldn't do any better than Lorett, that's for sure." Ms. Wilson tugged again at the dog and beamed at Alex.

He returned her smile feeling uncomfortable. In Vauseville, he probably couldn't find anyone better than Lorett, but the world was bigger than this speck on the map. Many of the women who had stayed here — the ones who hadn't left to pursue careers or find husbands in bigger cities — had few aspirations to do more than work at the local bank. Many struggled at home with children they had birthed in high school. Lorett was pretty and smart, managed the office for an accountant, and aspired to be an accountant herself one day.

He shifted closer to the door. "I should get back to work. You take care now." He squeezed his grandfather's shoulder as he stepped inside the store and counted the seconds before he could hear PawPaw make his escape from Ms. Wilson.

"I'd best be getting inside, too. My wife, you know Elaine, she's probably calling me for something right now."

As his grandfather came inside, he scowled at Alex, who found his grandfather's inability to flirt with another woman comical. "Now why you going to leave me out there with that woman when you know I can't stand her."

Alex tried to hide his laughter behind his hand. "She's hot for you, and you love it, PawPaw."

The old man rolled his eyes and grumbled his way into the back office, passing Richard who came out to see what the fuss was about.

"Mrs. Wilson?" Richard asked.

Alex affirmed his father's assumption with a smile.

For all the stories of Harper men being great warriors and leaders, few stories said much about their prowess with women. As far as he knew, PawPaw had always been a one-woman man. Elaine had been his high-school sweetheart and they had married quickly before Big Bear went off to fight in World War II, where he served with the 45th Army Infantry Division. To fight was his duty, he had said, to protect their life, liberty and land. Fifty years later, ironically, PawPaw was still fighting for his traditional way of life, for his people's liberty, and for their land. And all these years later, he was still married to his first and only love.

The notion that two people could be together for all those years amazed Alex.

～

THE LAKESIDE Restaurant and Bar smelled the same as always, like greasy fries left for days in a car when it's 90 degrees outside. Winston and Dave sat in their usual spot by the jukebox. Three empty beer bottles and two shot glasses were already lined up on the table. Alex surveyed the room before heading over to his old friends. The place wasn't crowded, yet. Lakeside was the only restaurant in Vauseville where anyone could get a beer with their dinner. George Capper and his wife, Zelda, owned the place and everyone teased them about the name, Lakeside, when it wasn't anywhere near a lake. People kept asking him: "When you putting in the lake, Cap?" Capper claimed he had been coming from North Carolina on his way to Lake Erie to set up his restaurant there, but got sidetracked when he spotted Zelda on the side of the road hitching a ride. She was on her way to Vauseville where her parents lived. That was forty years ago.

Capper stood behind the bar serving up beers with the speed of a man on vacation. Alex waved at him and the old man lifted an empty glass in salute. Winston stuck his fingers in his mouth and let loose a piercing whistle and Dave yelled, "Brother, what took you so long?"

They usually met up around seven; it was almost eight. The three men had grown up together in Vauseville, all from the same Bird Clan. Dave had married his high-school sweetheart but divorced a year later. These days, when he wasn't on a construction site, he was cuddling a bottle of Jack Daniels. Winston had met a Cherokee woman while he visiting his grandmother in Oklahoma. After two summer visits, Winston married her and brought her home. Five years later, they had three toddlers and one on the way. All three men were good with their hands, all artists in their own way. Dave would have been a master carpenter had he not dropped out of the program at the community college during his divorce. Winston had his own residential and commercial painting business. He also painted watercolors that he occasionally sold at festivals, but gave most away to friends and family as gifts.

A young woman dropped coins in the jukebox, filling the air with Garth Brooks and headed back to the dance floor where her partner stood waiting for her. Lucy, Capper's middle daughter, who now managed the restaurant for her parents, rushed over to Alex.

"It's always good to see you in Lakeside, Alex." She leaned forward and kissed his cheek letting her lips linger. Alex slid his hand around her waist and squeezed. "One of those days, sugar, you and me are gonna have some fun," she whispered.

Alex breathed in her sweet perfume and eyed the curve of her breasts beneath her low-cut top. "Next time your state trooper husband is out of town, you gimme a call," he said, and winked at her. Winston and Dave burst out laughing; Lucy winked back. Since they were all old enough to drink legally in the bar, Alex and Lucy had teased each other about one day sleeping together, although Alex had never taken her seriously, especially after she got married. He enjoyed the banter.

"You boys want another round?" she said. "And one for you too, sugar?"

Alex nodded. The couple on the dance floor moved languidly in each other's arms, clearly more interested in one another than in keeping the beat to the music. Alex looked around the place; Lakeside never changed. The large hall had a dozen tables dotted across the wooden floor; a small section was left open in the back for dancing. On Friday nights a local folk band played and a DJ came in on Saturdays. Zelda used to cook the dinners until it got too busy for her to keep up, so she hired a cook. People were scattered around, most of them eating the house burger and fries. Another couple was line dancing, and Little Man Thorpe, named so because he was six-foot-four, sat hunched over his drink in his usual spot at the end of the bar. Alex turned his attention to his friend Dave and asked him about his hair. The last time he had seen him, a week or so ago, Dave's hair had fallen past his shoulders. Now, it was shaved along the sides and back with a stretch of hair down the middle of his crown, tied in a short ponytail.

"I'm defying the stereotype of our people. The one you keep alive with your long ass hair. This is the look of the modern Indian."

"Defying a stereotype?" Alex laughed. "Sure your brother didn't do it one night while you were passed out drunk?"

Dave made an ugly face and pretended to laugh. He explained that his barber had come up with yet another bright idea for his client. Running his palm along the bare side of his head, Dave said, "I kinda like it."

Winston asked if Alex had heard about Little Jimmy Ross. Alex shook his head. Jimmy was a few years younger than him, nicknamed Little Jimmy to distinguish him from his father, Big Jimmy Ross, the second. Little Jimmy used to tease Alex that one day he was going to take Lorett away from Alex and marry her himself. "She ain't interested in you," Alex would say, but Jimmy would just smile and tell him to wait and see. Although all in jest, sometimes Alex wondered if maybe Lorett would be better off with Little Jimmy. He was dependable and could provide a steady life — that's all Lorett really wanted, wasn't it? After high school, Jimmy was promoted to manager of the motel along Fort Lewis Highway. A respectable establishment with more than one hundred rooms, not like the rooms-by-the-hour places just outside the city. Seemed like Jimmy was going to make something of himself. But he didn't.

"He got arrested last year for possession of amphetamines," Winston said. "Got caught up with a group of boys in Fort Lewis, distributing the drugs around Vauseville. He's serving a ten-year sentence in the pen."

Alex looked at his beer.

"And you remember his little brother, Sam?" Winston continued. "He's strung out on the drug. Been in and out of rehab since his brother got put away." Winston shook his head. "It's a damn shame."

There had been a few troublemakers from high school who had gone on to jail or been killed messing with the wrong people, but Alex couldn't fathom how Little Jimmy and his brother had landed on the same road as them. His people were in trouble with nothing to save them.

Lucy returned with a tray of beer bottles and set them down on the table.

"Hey Lucy, you hear Alex finally proposed to Lorett. He's gonna be off the market soon," said Dave.

"Yeah, I heard. That don't change a thing between us though," Lucy said, and blew a kiss at Alex before heading over to another table. The three men watched her skirt flick around her thick thighs as her high heels clicked across the room.

"Damn, I wish I could get a piece of that," Winston said. "I don't know why you don't just go ahead and tag it. You know she wants you."

Alex frowned. "You kidding? You know her husband, right? Chad Tilsen. He carries a gun on his days *off*. Besides, aren't you the happily married man? No need for you to be dreaming about some other woman."

Winston sucked down a mouthful of beer. "Happily and married don't necessarily go together, my friend."

"Bullshit!" said Dave. "You love your wife and wouldn't leave her if your life depended on it."

"That don't mean I can't be thinking about screwing another good-looking woman. As long as I don't follow my thoughts into action, it's all good."

"Seriously, Winston. You like being married?" Alex asked.

Winston surveyed the ceiling for a moment. "Yeah, I guess I do. The kids'll drive you crazy. But Tessa, she's the love of my life, my heart. And Dave's right, I'd die for her if I had to."

Alex couldn't respond and felt weighted by his friend's words as if the man had handed him a cinderblock. Would he ever love a woman enough to want to give his life for her? He vaguely remembered having such strong feelings for Lorett, back when he was a teenager, when life was a series of extreme highs and lows, and the world could end if he didn't have the right t-shirt for a party. He looked at Dave and remembered the empty expression on his face when he came over to the house to say Phoebe was kicking him out. At least five years had passed since then. She had said he didn't pay enough attention to her, that he was selfish and lazy, and didn't love her enough. Alex figured she was probably right on the lazy part, but all Dave had ever talked about was Phoebe — Alex couldn't imagine why she thought Dave didn't pay enough attention to her. Dave moved in with his baby brother and that's when he started drinking heavily and seemed to lose all sense of purpose.

Alex didn't want to get married only to end up in a divorce. Beyond sex, chocolate and babies, he had yet to grasp what made a woman happy.

"Lorett's been going on and on about you all getting married," Winston said. "She's been over at my sister's place looking at books and magazines on weddings."

Alex stared at the bottle in his hand. "Don't hold your breath."

Dave groaned. "That don't sound good."

"I don't think I'm ready for marriage. Too much responsibility."

"Yeah, well wait till you have kids," said Winston. "Man, life is one big responsibility. If we waited until we thought we were ready for something before we did it, nobody would do a damn thing. Seems to me it's more fun sharing those scary moments with someone else."

"Take it from me, brother, it ain't worth it," Dave said, his words beginning to slur. "Don't get married, especially if you're not ready. Women screw you over as soon as look at you. Trust me on that one."

Winston rolled his eyes. "We need to change the subject before Dave starts crying in his beer," he said. "Lucy, another round over here."

17

A LIGHT breeze rattled the old screens on the windows of Martha's kitchen, shifting the sweet smell of banana nut bread through the thick air. She pulled at her blouse in an attempt to cool herself, but the heat of the oven thwarted her effort. She settled onto a stool at the breakfast bar and read the letter she had received that morning from her sister. Mae had put her back out again and was stuck in bed for a few days. Martha chewed on her fingernail. She and her sister took turns calling each other about once a month and kept to a letter-writing tradition they had started after Mae first married and moved away from Fort Lewis. Martha had been in her last year at high school when Mae took off with her new husband to Baltimore. Five years later, she came back home, filing for a divorce. In no time, Mae found a new love and headed back to the courthouse for another marriage certificate. This one lasted two years. Finally, Mae met Buster, who was less flamboyant than the first two (one had owned a red Cadillac and the other had worn a diamond ring on each pinky). Buster was steady, much like the train company he worked for, and made her happy. They moved to Raleigh where they had remained ever since. Martha had yet to be third time lucky with love like her sister.

She scribbled a few words chiding Mae for not taking better care of herself, then ended the sentence with a large smiley face. As Martha wrote, she heard her daughter's familiar light tapping at the back door, which squeaked open then clicked closed. Kira quietly stepped into the kitchen. Her daughter's moan of joy as she smelled the banana bread tickled Martha. She welcomed her in, returning the hug and kiss Kira pressed into her hot cheek before taking a seat at the table.

"I'm glad you came by," Martha said. "I've been worried about you."

"I'm okay."

Martha suspected her daughter was still angry. "Look, I'm sorry—"

"Let's not talk about it, okay?" Kira said, looking at the table. "Not yet."

They chattered about Mae and her back problems. Martha wanted to visit her sister this weekend but worried that her car wouldn't make the journey; it likely needed a new muffler. Kira's suggestion that they drive down together surprised her.

"You mean you'd give up your fun-filled weekend to hang out with me? No Jamal?"

"He can wait. Besides, you need to get out more and do something fun instead of staying cooped up in here like some old woman."

Martha frowned. Kira asked when she had last been to a party, other than some gathering at the church. Martha stared at her notepaper. She couldn't remember the last time she had been to a party, a real party with good music and dancing. For a millionth time that day, she thought of Larry and the parties they had attended together. Had Kira called him? His phone call had stirred up memories that should have been lost forever, memories of slow dancing and long kisses. Martha felt the familiar sting of indigestion. Trying to change the subject, she asked about Kira's day. She gathered loose pages and tapped the thin stack on the table before neatly laying the pile flat. She pressed her palm between her breasts feeling her chest burn. Sliding off the stool, she went to the refrigerator, poured milk into a tumbler and gulped it down. Milk was better than any antacid she had ever bought. If only it would take away her memories. She had been thinking about those days, when the papers were filled with boycotts and marches across the country and people getting arrested simply for standing up for what they believed in. She remembered the shock that had rippled through countless homes when Martin Luther King Jr. was killed. Everything changed then. Before that, Martha didn't recall any uprisings in her neighborhood, although it seemed to be happening everywhere else. In fact, where she lived, while segregation was in full effect, an undercurrent of togetherness prevailed between some blacks and whites from what she could tell. Or, maybe it was just at the club where she met Larry. Blacks and whites mingled freely there. Being with Larry had made her feel hopeful about the world, that maybe the two races could live together in peace. Although it wasn't so bad then, not really. Looking at the TV news, it did seem like the world was on fire, but not in the Midnight Club.

Sniffing the air, she remembered the loaf. "Oh goodness, I'm gonna burn this bread." She gently lowered herself from the stool and grabbed the two padded mittens from the counter. The oven's heat smarted her cheeks. The top of the bread was crisp. Shaking the loaf from the pan, she rolled it upright on a round plate, then took a knife from the drawer and laid everything on the table below her daughter's nose. "Now, let it cool before you go digging in it."

Kira ignored the warning and cut a crumbly slice. Her mother resettled herself on her stool and watched Kira's face squint as she burned her tongue. Undaunted, Kira continued to nibble, her face shaped just like her father's — the slope of her forehead and the roundness of her chin. Her expressions also were her father's, and Martha saw it clearly now in Kira's concentration as she worked on the bread.

"Did you, uh, call—?"

Kira didn't look up but responded with a firm, "No."

"Oh." Martha looked away and adjusted her already neat stack of writing paper. "Are you going to?"

Kira shrugged. She nibbled at the crumbs on her plate. "There's a lot going on right now. I'm just not sure. He's a stranger to me, Ma." She paused then looked up at her mother. "Why didn't you ever tell me the truth about him?"

Martha kept silent. His sudden re-appearance had unsettled her, and she scolded herself for keeping the truth from her daughter. She hadn't meant to hide Larry Walsh, but neither had she wanted to encourage his existence in their lives. While she accepted blame, he had made little effort as a father in the almost thirty years since Kira's birth, and Larry was foolish to expect Kira to open her arms to him. Until his phone call, Martha thought she had made peace with that period of her life, but now it hung loosely out from the seams, exposing her bad attempt to tuck everything neatly away.

"I'm sorry for all this. I truly am," she said. She wanted to sound sincere, wanted Kira to know how much she regretted not being completely honest. "I never thought he would ever appear in our lives again. I guess I told you he was killed in the war 'cause maybe that's what I wanted to believe. That's what I wanted to be true."

"I wish he had been."

"Sweetheart, don't think that way. I'm not sure about all this myself, but I do know God has a plan and this must be part of it."

She stroked her daughter's cheek and thought about the adage that what doesn't kill you, makes you stronger. Only, right now she couldn't have felt more weak.

"It's like I'm not really who I thought I was," said Kira. "Does that make sense?" Lines creased her forehead and Martha tried to wipe them away with her fingers.

"We were both so young back then. We had no idea what having a baby was all about. But I have *never* regretted having you. Never."

"I did just fine without him."

"Yes. Yes you did."

Martha was proud that her little girl had grown into an intelligent and independent woman. At the same age, Martha had been the mother of a five-year-old. Getting pregnant just as she had established herself as a responsible young nurse at the hospital almost destroyed her career. And carrying a child by a white man filled her with dread — while there may have been an undercurrent of togetherness, in reality the country was in turmoil over race relations. More importantly, she knew her father would be furious both at her irresponsibility and at being with a white man.

Martha had taken a bus to Baltimore to tell her sister and had spent the weekend agonizing over telling her parents. Mae gave her the support she needed, neither chastising her nor telling her to get rid of the baby. Although Mae did encourage her to tell the baby's father, Martha was reluctant to do so. Her parents, however, she had to tell.

Martha told her mother then burst into tears and sobbed through the remainder of that Sunday evening, consumed by fear. When her father finally came home from a meeting of the church deacons, she repeated her news. He had stared at her, stone faced, for a long time. Her father had been a big man, standing at almost six-feet-four with a voice that could compete with a bass drum. Although a gentle man, when angered he was an imposing figure to reckon with. Martha couldn't look at him anymore and stood feeling like a cockroach he was about to squash. Finally, in a steady tone he told her to pack her things and leave. Her mother protested, but he left the kitchen and took his place in his comfy chair, newspaper in hand. There was no need in pleading with him — his decision had been made.

Martha got permission from her boss to take a six-month leave of absence. She stayed with Mae and gave birth in Baltimore. In the meantime, Martha's mother helped find a two-roomed apartment in Fort Lewis and watched the baby while Martha returned to her nursing job at the hospital. She never, not for one moment, considered getting rid of the child, but those first few years were a struggle, and more often than not she fantasized about calling Larry and demanding his help and his money. Mae had phoned him, so he knew about the baby, but it was two years before he called to say his tour in Nam was over and that he wanted to be a daddy. Confused and afraid, Martha shut him out. She was on good terms with her own father again, and knew she had to choose between Kira's white father and her own strict father. She chose her own.

Bluntly, she told Larry Walsh she didn't need him and didn't want him in their lives. It pained her now remembering her harsh words, and his soft voice asking why, promising to be a good father, apologizing for not contacting her before shipping out. After that phone call, she never heard from him again.

At times, Martha wished she had been more responsible and had never gotten caught up in his sweet talk in the first place. Yet, because she had allowed herself to love him, she had a beautiful daughter. That truth confirmed for her that all things happen for a reason known only to God.

"Does anyone besides Mae know about him?" her daughter asked.

"No one who's living anymore."

Martha let her mind wander back to when she first met Larry Walsh. He wasn't especially good looking, but he had a charming way about him. "He was such a smooth talker," she said. "They called him Double T back then because he could play the trumpet twice as good as anyone else." She rolled her eyes and smiled at her daughter. Memories engulfed her as if a dam holding them back had ruptured.

"He played the trumpet?" Kira's eyes brightened again.

While the bitterness of being alone with a newborn had weighed her down, Martha couldn't help but laugh at her days dancing at the Midnight Club where Larry played with a jazz band, which drew a mixed crowd. Two members of the popular five-piece band were white. She told Kira about the club and the group of friends she and her sister had gone with every Friday night. During the breaks between sets, Larry would come and talk to her. He had taken a liking to her for reasons she never did understand. He was as white as they come, with short blonde hair and intense blue eyes that captured her gaze one night and never let go. Most of the time, when he played, he kept those eyes closed with his entire body bending with the trumpet's notes as they lulled then screamed at the audience. One night, while the saxophonist had the lead, Martha had spotted Larry talking and laughing with the drummer. He spied her watching him and as soon as the next break came, he was at her table asking her name and if she liked the music.

"Of course I like the music. I wouldn't be here otherwise," she said, laughing.

"I haven't seen you here before. Is this your first visit?"

"Nope. I come here every Friday with my sister, Mae, when she's in town. She's the one talking to your drummer."

"I've met Mae before. She didn't tell me she had a sister prettier than anyone I've ever seen before in my life."

Martha blushed. "In your life?"

"That's what I said." He pressed his finger to his chin and thought for a moment. "Yep. I'd say I'm right. Never seen anyone prettier in my life."

He asked what her favorite instrument was, and when she said the bass guitar he feigned a stab to his heart.

"Then it's my goal to make you fall in love with the trumpet," he said. And in the weeks that followed, Martha fell in love with more than the music.

In a hotel room on the outskirts of town, she kissed his tanned shoulder and let him undress her. Although not her first lover, he was the most gentle and considerate man to ever touch her. They never discussed marriage. While she cared for him deeply, she knew she didn't have the fight in her to make a mixed marriage work. When they spent time together, at the club or alone, they simply stayed in the present moment. Getting pregnant had never been a consideration, and the doctor's pronouncement shocked Martha. She couldn't face going to the club any more and because she had made it clear that he never call the house for fear her father pick up the phone, she succeeded in avoiding him.

"Sometimes the Lord says it's not meant to be and sets us on different paths," she had told Kira all those years ago. "The Lord brought your father and me together to create you, but He had different plans for us that meant we can't be together. He took your daddy up to Heaven with him." She hadn't planned to lie. In fact, Martha hadn't planned what to say to her daughter at all. The words were the first that came to mind and slipped out as if they had been waiting just for that moment. And once out, she wasn't sure how to take them back, especially when her daughter accepted the answer, placing faith in her mother's lie. But Martha had lived with the guilt. It awakened her in the night, yet with each passing year, as Kira's questions faded away, it became easier to pretend that the lie was the truth, easier to let him disappear, to believe he was dead, and let the truth get buried beneath each new day. As the years passed, she found a new love. What she thought was love. Martha had yet to forgive herself for making the same mistake all over again.

Jim was a sweet-talking welder who worked at the factory. They had met at Hal's diner where they both stopped for breakfast on their way to work each morning. They both worked the seven-to-three shift and would chat while they waited for their takeout orders. Eventually he asked her out, which panicked her because years had passed since she had been on a date. But she accepted. Jim started out being considerate and thoughtful — calling to ask about her day, sending her cards and fixing her old car when it broke down. They dated for several months before Martha gave in to his pleas and brought him to her bed. Six weeks later, when her period didn't come, a pregnancy test confirmed her fear. Martha hoped he would be happy, hoped he wanted a family, that he wanted to spend the rest of his life with her and Kira. She was banking on the time they had spent together, enjoying each other's company, on the flowers and the kisses he had given her. Only, he was far from happy. He was livid. He shouted at her for being so reckless, for trapping him. Too shocked to cry, she stood dumbfounded as he berated her for being irresponsible. He wasn't ready for a family, wasn't ready to settle down or be married. He didn't want that life, but he would do the right thing, he said. He would marry her, for the sake of the child, he said.

They had a quick wedding at the courthouse. She wore a pale pink dress she had worn at Mae's first wedding. The layers of chiffon made her feel especially feminine. In the Justice of the Peace's office, she stood next to Jim, her heart thudding in her throat. Not until prompted to say, "I do" did she feel panic. In that split moment she almost walked out. But she said the words, all the while hoping it would all work out for the best. It surprised her that he didn't hesitate, saying the two little words with confidence. He kissed her firmly and held her hand as they walked back to the car. She was hopeful. They rented a cramped two-bedroom house on Railroad Avenue. Less than two years into the marriage, Martha woke up one day and Jim had already left the house. She assumed he had gone to work early, but he didn't come home for dinner. His chicken plate sat warming in the oven. When she called the plant, the floor supervisor said Jim had quit a week ago. Martha crawled into bed and stayed there for several days, sleeping away hour after hour and ignoring her daily chores and bills. Her mother brought food and got little Kira off to school in the mornings then sat with Martha, rocking the toddler, reading scripture and praying. Finally, she brought a minister to counsel her child. Over time, Martha began to understand that with Jesus Christ she could be forgiven and begin anew.

The first time she received a check in the mailbox from Jim for a hundred dollars, she almost ripped it to shreds. Then a few months after that, another check arrived and more came periodically. When Kenny was around three years old, his father began to visit, and Martha began hoping again. But it didn't last. The visits and the money eventually stopped coming altogether. Martha vowed no man would ever hurt her again. She gave herself to the Lord — reading the Bible every morning and vowing to follow a righteous path — and focused her energy on raising her children.

The screech of tires on the street outside shook the air and Martha thanked God that wasn't her son. The kitchen had begun to cool now although the banana fragrance lingered in the atmosphere. She looked at Kira, feeling blessed that both her children had grown into well-adjusted, intelligent young people.

"How do you feel about Larry Walsh now?" Kira asked.

Martha considered the question for a moment then said, "I

won't say I have no regrets, but perhaps this was meant to happen. I've been hiding from it all these years and now it's time for me to face my past, and for you to discover your beginning."

~

KIRA LOOKED at the phone number for Larry Walsh. Who was this man who had charmed her mother? Who had played the trumpet in a jazz band and had mixed with blacks when it wasn't considered appropriate for the time? Was he like Miles cool? Did he travel the world playing for jazz greats? Did he meet Coltrane? Maybe he wasn't a bad guy, after all. He had been nothing but a ghost for all her years growing up, and now he was alive — she had heard his voice at the other end of the telephone. Perhaps this *was* a chance to discover the other half of herself she had never known. To know this white man, perhaps, would be to know herself more fully. *This white man.* Gingerly, she dialed the number and waited. Deja vu.

"Hello?" A man's voice, his voice. She shook and her throat was closing. Again, he spoke. "Hello?"

She swallowed a lump. "Yes. Hello. This is Kira."

His voice was small-town Southern with a nasal edge to it like Willie Nelson as he said how glad he was that she had called him back. He thought she had decided against the idea.

"I had. But I . . . It seemed, you know, like I should."

"I just want to know you. Make a few wrongs right."

Words jumbled around her head and she grasped at them, randomly accepting one then immediately rejecting it. The two words that kept banging against the inside of her forehead were: "Why now?" They spilled out before she realized she had said anything. His voice stumbled; he wasn't sure. She had never truly left his thoughts, he said. She had remained a silent shadow, a vague question mark in the shape of a little girl who grew a darker gray with every year. He wanted to know what she was like, if she anything like him? "I got no other children," he said.

No other children. It dawned on her that she could have had a slew of white siblings, then like a bat across her head she realized he was acknowledging that he was her father, and suddenly everything her mother had said was real, the Midnight Club, the trip to Baltimore. She was talking to her father. What was she supposed to say? He asked if he could meet her, suggested meeting for coffee. "Do you drink coffee?"

She nodded, then realized he couldn't see her, but she couldn't speak. Couldn't scream at him to go away and leave her alone. Couldn't jump the clock back so she had known about him all along. Couldn't jump forward so all this would be behind her. She could hear him breathing, patiently waiting for her response. Her curiosity got the best of her, so she agreed. He suggested Dee's Deli on Chapel Street, downtown at eleven o'clock. She had two hours before she would finally see her real, flesh-and-blood father. After she hung up, Kira stared at the telephone for a long time.

When he sat opposite her in the restaurant, his smile revealed a dimple that dented his left cheek. His face looked like it had been scrubbed clean with a brush and his cheeks shone a rosy pink above the ragged line of a beard that hadn't yet grown full. His crooked white teeth were small like a child's, a few freckles dotted his Roman nose, and tiny flecks of silver sparkled in his bright blue eyes giving him a boyish innocence. His fair wavy hair almost reached his shoulders, and he wore a denim shirt under an old Army jacket. He smelled of stale liquor, tobacco and soap. He's a redneck, she thought. There was no sign of the cool trumpet player her mother had talked about. Maybe her story of him had been another lie. Kira found it difficult to correlate his white features with the father she had imagined him to be; neither could she connect this face to her own. Larry fidgeted with the salt and pepper shakers and laid a pack of Marlboro cigarettes together with a plastic lighter on the table next to the No Smoking sign. She remembered when she had attempted smoking for the first time in high school with some friends in the girls' bathroom. She had gotten nauseous and sat with her head over the toilet seat dry heaving for an eternity. Kira bit the skin around her nails. She had a habit of chewing the hang nail, then moving on to the ragged skin around it. Her front teeth nibbled on the inside of her lips, pulling away any loose strand of skin she caught. She felt the tension in her jaw and struggled to control her compulsion by firmly pressing her teeth together, only it didn't feel comfortable and she quickly lapsed back into her nibbling. Could Larry Walsh tell that her heart was beating double-time? She wiped her clammy palms on a napkin and breathed deeply to calm herself. It helped that she could see he was just as nervous, maybe more so than she. He smiled uneasily at her, perhaps waiting for her to make the first move.

"You're much prettier than I imagined," he said, finally.

Kira looked at the steam swirling upward from her coffee cup, resenting his compliment. *Ma never told me you were white*, she wanted to say, but instead she said, "So you served in Vietnam?"

Larry's smile faded and he looked away for a moment. Kira clung to the table to stop her hands from shaking and mentally kicked herself.

After a while he said, "I served in the Marines and did two tours in Vietnam."

"Ma said you were dead."

He raised his eyebrows then sipped his black coffee. "Can't say I blame her for that."

He began chewing on the inside of his cheek and Kira realized they were both doing the same thing. She stopped immediately. Watching him, she didn't like what she saw. Didn't want to see herself in him. This wasn't the man she had dreamed her father to be. This man was a redneck truck driver who screwed around with her mother and left. He had no right to come back into her life now, almost thirty years later. He cleared his throat and took a long gulp of his drink. He said she looked just like her mother. "You got her eyes." A tiny diamond sparkled in his left ear as he moved. "I wanted to be there every minute for you. But you and your mom, you know, you were better off."

"Without you?" He gazed at her with caring and warmth, yet Kira's resentment continued to rise. He sat there, saying kind words, but for all those years had made no effort to see her, and so many years ago he could have changed her belief that he was dead with one phone call, one letter.

He nodded, yes.

"You think so?" she said, studying him as he studied her. Was he trying to gauge her feelings?

"It was Mae who called me with the news. Told me Martha was having a baby and I was the daddy. I didn't know what to do. I figured she didn't want me involved no how cause she never called me herself. But hey, I move with the wind. Not quite the family man. And mixed relationships, you know, they can be tough. I didn't want your mom to go through that bullshit. Excuse my French." He looked right into her eyes. "I never stopped thinking about you, about you both. I shouldn't have stayed away, but we was young, and it just seemed easier that way."

Kira lifted her coffee cup with both hands hoping it wouldn't shake and took a sip. She held the cup below her chin, her arms blocking her chest like a boxer protecting herself from another blow. Most men were easy to manipulate, but this one was different. This man had been her mother's lover, and she didn't know how to react.

"When I finally got the gumption to call and try to be a daddy, well, your mother rightly told me where to go. I don't blame her for that," he said. "I shouldn't have used her words as an excuse to disappear. I know that now. But you've been on my mind." He paused. "Can you forgive me?"

Forgiveness? Is that what he wanted? Kira looked at the stranger sitting across from her. She felt uncomfortable with his question and said nothing. He looked at the table and started twisting the cigarette lighter in his hand. "You need to talk to my mother," she said, her voice sharp now. "She's the one who should forgive you. She's the one you hurt."

"I'm the last person on earth your mother wants to see. I don't think me saying sorry will change nothing for her. But you . . . you still have your whole life ahead of you, and I don't want you to hate me for the rest of it." He swallowed. "Maybe I'm getting old and trying to make peace with the past, but I want you to know, I'm just a guy who made some mistakes."

"You can't make it all better with a cup of coffee."

He thought for a moment. "It's a start."

A start to what? She had grown up without a father. She had figured out the birds and the bees and had learned how to deal with men without him. She had learned to drive, had graduated high school and college, established a career and bought her own home. What good was a father to her now?

"I don't need you." She stood up abruptly and left him sitting in the deli. She strode into the street, where the heat took away her breath and burned her face.

18

KIRA WELCOMED the hot sun on her skin, hoping it would melt the chill she felt inside. Instead of going to her car, she walked to the little bookstore on the corner of Main and Bridge Street. She enjoyed this place when she didn't know what else to do. Books were reliable. Alphabetized and orderly, their familiar titles offered comfort. She could find a new world in the fiction section, laugh at the ridiculous romance novels (as if love were ever that simple) and find advice from a psychologist on whatever was bothering her. She had searched through hardback and soft-cover books, trying to discover how to find a reliable, loving man, but more so trying to figure out what love was really all about. Now, as she wandered through the aisles, through the crisp smell of new pages and the musty oak shelves, she wondered if there was a book on absent fathers who come back into their daughters' lives after a lifetime of separation. What was she supposed to feel? Or do?

The bookstore appeared empty except for the thin man flipping through a cookbook behind the cash register. As she tiptoed across the wooden floor, she turned a corner and saw him sitting on a low stool. His black hair fell loose and hid his face as he peered into an oversized book. He wore brown leather cowboy boots with deep scuffmarks that had darkened with age. Faded blue jeans covered his long legs. His ragged nature appealed to her. A casual confidence — was he even aware of it? — made him intriguing. She wanted to touch his hair, slide her hand over his thigh, press her fingers against his chest, stroke her lashes across his cheek, and capture his breath into her own. Instead, she backed quietly away, but her arm bumped the bookshelf and Alex looked up. His slim fingers raked through his hair and he smiled, squinting at her, his greeting hanging in the air. She felt unsettled, as if he had caught her peeking at a private moment between lovers. He stood up, holding the large book out like a tray and slowly their words began, soft, simple, warming the air and dissipating their awkwardness. He slid the book — a history of American art — back into an open slot on the shelf, stuffed his hands in his pockets, and gazed at her.

"Do you have time to get lunch?" he asked.

PEOPLE CROWDED the sandwich shop across the street but the line moved quickly. Alex and Kira found a table near the back and this time their conversation came easily. He asked her what got her into the newspaper business. Telling him "to make a difference" sounded trite, and it seemed so long ago since she had made the decision to become a journalist that she wasn't sure of the real reason anymore. She liked writing but didn't want to teach, and journalism seemed practical, she explained. She could earn a living writing and doing things she wouldn't normally do, like attending a powwow and a spiritual Indian dance.

"You could have danced with us," Alex said. He watched her closely, studying her face. She could see his eyes moving, looking at her hair, her nose, her mouth. "Why didn't you dance with us?"

She didn't know what to say. That it wasn't her culture, it wasn't who she was? And now, she wondered why she had chosen a career that always had her on the outside looking in. Is that where she found life more comfortable, watching others live their lives while she sat on the bench?

"I'm a journalist," she said. "We're supposed to be objective observers. But the truth is, I can't dance."

Alex chuckled. "I thought all black people could dance? Isn't that what they say?" Was he teasing her? He leaned forward, closer to her. "People are too self conscious. You just move to the sound. Let the beat grab you inside, and move."

"Is that like your art? It grabs you inside?"

"That's a good way to put it. I suppose it does."

He talked about his time in Albuquerque, his dark eyes brightening as he described the paintings he saw, the sculptures, the drawings, art in all its forms, traditional, contemporary, he loved it all. "The greatest thing about the school was learning Indian art history, and the different styles from different tribes. I came to appreciate the beauty of the Indian people as a whole."

"You are beautiful." Instantly, she wanted to pull the words back into her mouth. "I mean, your … your people are beautiful, your culture." He gave her a wicked grin. She changed the subject and asked him what he thought of the paper. "Honestly?" Yes, honestly. His response was lukewarm as he looked at his sandwich. She reassured him that he wouldn't hurt her feelings if he didn't like it.

"It's not that I don't like it," he said. "For a regional paper it's just so . . . so boring!" He laughed and apologized. "Maybe I'm not interested in the local stuff that happens around here, but there are never any surprises. It's always the same formula stuff — bland stories about our government leaders and community organizers, all white, all pushing their own agendas that most of the time, I don't care much about." He smiled. "Really, the paper's fine. I'm just not interested, I guess. Now PawPaw, on the other hand, he reads it religiously every day and pores over it on Sundays. Your story will be the first on our community that he can remember."

"That doesn't surprise me. The newspaper is still stuck in the fifties. Racism smolders inside people until something ignites it, then it comes raging out. They think one story on Native Americans or one story featuring a black person makes up for years and years of nothing at all." Glancing at her watch, she realized her mid-morning break to meet Larry Walsh had turned into a three-hour lunch.

Outside, the heat still clung to the concrete although the sun had moved across the sky creating long shadows on the ground.

Kira stood with Alex on the sidewalk for a moment in silence. She scrambled around in her purse to find a business card and handed it to him. "You can always reach me at the paper."

"Does it have to be work-related?" With a wink at her, Alex slipped the card into his back pocket and left her standing alone in the street.

"Not at all," she whispered.

～

THE BLOCK felt heavy. Alex moved the wood from one hand to the other, feeling the rough grain against his skin. Instead of going straight home, he had stopped at the lumber yard along Fort Lewis highway where the foreman there, an old friend from high school, put aside discarded wood blocks for Alex. He sat on a boulder by Deer Creek in the afternoon sun studying the fine piece of maple he had pulled from the pile and considered what he would create. He closed his eyes and listened to the rush of the water, the breeze shivering the leaves around him, and felt the weight resting in his palms. When he opened his eyes a blue heron stood statuesque, one foot in the water, and then shifted in slow motion before stopping again, its gaze on the small fish below the surface. Alex captured every detail of the bird he could in his mind, pulled his penknife from his pocket and began to chip away at the wood.

The afternoon faded into evening and he could hear the mosquitoes starting to buzz and the crickets beginning to call, the heron long gone. When his stomach rumbled, he decided to leave. Buoyed by his new creation — still in rough form — he bounded into his grandparents' home ready to share his joy with anyone who would listen. But as soon as he entered the sitting room, his father leaped from a chair and lashed out at him.

"Where the hell have you been?" Paw was not a man to curse, but a string of obscenities flowed from his lips. Alex stood silent as his father raged, his face darker than a red apple, asking repeatedly, "Where were you?" but giving no space for Alex to respond. MawMaw stood mute in the doorway between the kitchen and the sitting room, clutching a dish towel to her chest. Alex could hear his PawPaw behind him say, "Richard, let the boy explain himself."

Alex felt the blood rush to his feet when he realized what he had done. It was today. The Blessing Ceremony was today. Members of each clan, Alex's Bird Clan and Lorett's Deer Clan, were to gather with the priest to officially bless the engagement and consent to the eventual marriage union. A feast was planned at the community center, a feast that MawMaw and the elder Bird Clan women, had prepared. How could he have forgotten?

"I thought it was tomorrow," he said when Richard finally fell silent.

"Tomorrow?" His father's chest heaved and in an instant Alex felt the sting of his father's hand across his cheek. "You're an embarrassment to me and to this family."

MawMaw shrieked and admonished Richard for striking her grandson. Suddenly Alex was eleven again feeling his father's hand smack his face because he had made his family late to his brother's induction into the Boy Scouts' Order of the Arrow. Alex had taken off that morning and lost track of time. His excuse had been the same as today — he had forgotten. His father had called him selfish and inconsiderate, words he said to him now. No other time had his father struck him in anger.

Alex stared at the floor, anger rising in his stomach, anger at his father. He hated him, hated trying to be the leader and family man his father wanted him to be, hated making wedding plans to satisfy his father. Alex was wading outside the realm of his own desires to please this man who only saw his son's failures. He felt the weight of the wooden sculpture in his grip and raising his arm high, he brought it down quickly, smashing the bird into the floor. He would not let his father rule him anymore. He turned to escape the room but Big Bear blocked his path.

"We must make amends," PawPaw said. His fists tight against his thighs, Alex struggled to contain the urge to punch down the door and escape into the night. He knew he had messed up. How could he have been so stupid? This time he had failed not only his father, but his entire clan and had disrespected Lorett and her family. He didn't want to face his grandfather or anyone else, but he knew he had to. It was the right thing to do. He swallowed a tight knot in his throat.

Carrying the covered dishes from the dinner, Alex took them to Lorett's home where many of her family members were gathered. Her eyes were puffy from tears and immediately he wanted to fall into a deep hole rather than face her and everyone else. With his grandparents at his back, he stood discomfited before the Deer Clan and recited the words of apology that MawMaw had helped him prepare. He knelt before his fiancée and asked for her forgiveness, all the while wishing he could sprout wings and fly away into the clouds.

THE SUN had barely risen and Elaine moved through the house watering her houseplants, talking to them as if they were old friends. Alex looked at her through the screen door as she stroked the leaves of a fern. Since Alex was in second grade, she had been the only woman in the family, the woman who had mothered him. Memories of his mother were vague, a blurred face behind hands reaching out to him, a sad sensation emanating from her embrace, cold tears staining his cheek. When he could, he would squirm and wriggle away to MawMaw's arms, which wrapped him in warm love. Elaine had been a young bride and gave birth to three boys — only the middle child, Richard, survived past childbirth. Alex wondered if the family was jinxed in some way — almost every Harper generation had been touched by an early death.

Sleep had come to him in spurts through the night and he awakened before dawn. Rather than stare at the dark, he headed out to run. The air was cool as he ran through the main street and turned onto the trail into the woods off Juniper Lane. The smell of pine from the towering trees lifted his mood as his feet pounded the hard dirt along the path. All night he had thought of Lorett, of marriage, of his father's rage. Now, he let his mind empty and refill with the peace of his surroundings. He followed the trail for about three miles and came out near his grandparent's house where he caught MawMaw with her plants. He crept inside.

"Do they talk back?" he said, giving her a hug from behind.

Elaine reached up and pressed her palm into his cheek. "You devil," she said, and kissed his face. "Sometimes it's the best conversation I get." She put the watering can on the floor and asked how he was feeling.

Alex shrugged. "Where's PawPaw?"

"He went fishing with your Paw. Said they were bringing home dinner, but I took some brisket out the freezer, just in case."

Relieved that he wouldn't have to face his father quite yet, Alex went upstairs for a quick shower before returning to the kitchen and treating his MawMaw to breakfast. He busied himself at the stove, pleased to be giving her a break, although she insisted on preparing the coffee and hovered over him, making sure he was fluffing the eggs the way she had taught him and crisping the bacon just so.

"You'll make a wonderful husband, Alex." She hushed his protest and told him not to be hard on himself. "We'll get past this."

"Lorett will never let me live this down."

"For some girls, marriage is their chance to step out of the shadow of their mothers, to be in charge of their own lives, their own households, and to have babies to pass on their ways. Whether it's fair or not, Lorett's put all her hopes in you for a better life." Elaine squeezed his arm. "Just as you're afraid of getting sucked into a life you don't want, she's equally afraid of getting stuck in the life she's in now."

He had never considered that he represented a way for Lorett to escape her own life. She lived with her mother and helped care for her ailing grandmother who also lived in their two-story wooden frame house. Her two younger brothers had moved to California during the three years Alex had been gone. Most of their generation had moved away to bigger cities seeking better job opportunities. The desperation in those left behind created currents in the air for the birds to soar farther and farther away. He wished he had stayed away.

"But don't let all this stunt your ambition."

"Ambition?"

His ambition was reflected in his creativity, she said, and in his desire to seek out new experiences. "Don't let anyone squeeze that out of you. Now let's eat."

19

KIRA SKIMMED past the front section of the Sunday paper, past the opinions, sports and local news until she found the features section. The paper's musty smell of paper and ink caught in her throat, making her cough. She expected to see her story on the Harpers and their struggle to raise money to buy their ancestral lands above the fold on page one of the Features section. She had imagined the top half showing a colorful picture of Alex in the midst of his dance and couldn't wait to see what pictures Pete had selected. Instead, the crumpled face of an elderly white man wearing a ball-cap with an old gas station behind him stared back at her. She looked at the byline — Mark Livingstone, her coworker. She straightened out the paper, spreading it across the kitchen table and looked at the whole front page. Her story appeared nowhere on the section's front. She licked her fingers and opened the pages, looking at each one carefully. Finally, she found it on the next-to-last page opposite the movie listings, and sank with disappointment. No picture of Alex, just one small black and white picture of Big Bear sitting at the booth. And to her horror the caption identified him as Richard Harper. A long guttural groan escaped her. While not much of the story had been cut, it was squeezed into two columns, buried inside the paper. She seethed, letting her voice fill the room as she raged about why her story had gotten shafted; she would call the editor and demand to know what happened; she would take the issue to Barker, the managing editor, and ask that it be rerun. For so many reasons, this was an important story and should have gotten better play in the paper. The inside back page was a death zone for any piece — a spread on the back page, though not great, would have been better. She looked at the cover story on the old man, who at 90 still ran the gas station he had opened fifty years earlier. Big deal. She called Beverly and ranted: was it that she was black, that the photographer was black? Was it because the story focused on Native Americans? Or was it that the entire city desk consisted of whites, and mostly white men at that, who saw no significance in offering diversity in the paper's pages? Or maybe the editors had a reasonable explanation that had nothing to do with race.

"Girl, I hate to say it, but you and I both know there's no reasonable explanation here," said Beverly. "Even if it wasn't about race, it still wouldn't make it reasonable."

"Why is it that after all these years, we're still struggling to be heard? Surely it's not like this everywhere?"

"Fort Lewis is always a few steps behind the rest of the world. Maybe at a bigger paper you wouldn't have to deal with this mess."

Maybe. The desire to leave Fort Lewis came surging back. She wanted to go to a new city, a new paper, and create a new life for herself. She should have left Fort Lewis years ago, if not for the responsibility she felt to be near her mother. Maybe the time to go was now.

"But we grew up in this town," said Beverly. "If we don't care what happens here, who will?"

～

Alex savored the iced tea Lorett had given him. He loved her mother's iced tea: sweet with just a hint of lemon. He leaned back in the lounge chair on the porch and breathed in the warm evening air. He had brought her meat and vegetables — a Cherokee tradition that symbolized his role as caretaker of her and her family — his effort to make amends, to express his love and attention. He had been forgiven, but another ceremony had to be scheduled before the Deer Clan would officially consent to the wedding. Without a blessing from both clans, the wedding could not take place.

The night heat made his skin moist and he imagined the joy of slipping off his clothes and sliding into a lake. "Let's go skinny dipping," he said. Lorett rolled her eyes and said nothing. He pictured the short summer dress she wore falling to her feet and feeling her body against his in the water. "I'm serious. We can go up to Wapato Lake. It's only twenty minutes away."

She told him to stop being ridiculous. There were snakes in that lake. Alex protested, but she continued to list reasons they shouldn't go, not the least of which was the likelihood they would get caught and arrested for indecent exposure.

"Besides, I'm tired," she said.

Alex didn't wear a watch but guessed it couldn't be later than eight. He finished his drink, placed the glass on the floor and let out a burp. Lorett admonished him for not excusing himself. He nodded, acknowledging her comment, but kept quiet.

"We should go to the movies," she said. "There's a cool action movie opening that I want to see. We could go with Winston and Tessa."

Every time he sat in a movie theatre for two hours, Alex felt his life draining away into the cushioned seat. He would rather be drawing or sculpting, or doing nothing outdoors where the fresh air seemed to fill him with new life. He suggested they go for a walk. She wanted to know where. He shrugged. "Deer Creek." Neither of them moved as if the effort would deplete their energy reserves. Lorett began recounting a story about her co-worker who had recently married and honeymooned in Hawaii. The co-worker had gotten food poisoning and had to be rushed to the hospital. Alex noticed a cut log on the ground near the house; the flat surface revealed the rings of the tree's many years, which had ended with the swiftness of a chainsaw. How many generations had seen this tree grow, he wondered. In the waning light, the log's lines appeared to wiggle, moving gently as if pushed by a breeze. He saw his father's face in the lines and his grandfather and his brother, their long hair floating around them. His own face appeared. Alex stared at the apparition.

"Isn't that funny?" Lorett said.

His attention snapped back to her. Funny? She had said her co-worker had gotten sick. What had he missed that was funny? "I just remembered something," he said and stood up. "I'll call you later."

He could hear her calling after him but the image sharpened in his brain and he didn't want to lose it. He held the vision of the faces in his mind as he strode the half-mile back to his apartment above the shop. There, he immediately found his drawing pad and pencil and scribbled the picture from his memory. Four faces. Three generations. He would carve the picture into wood.

20

*T*HE *CHEROKEE people had been forced out of Southwest Virginia in the late 1700s when settlers were claiming the land for themselves. Many had died in the numerous territorial battles along the frontier. Those who survived moved west to Tennessee and on to Oklahoma or south to the Carolinas. My people went to North Carolina and lived there peacefully for many years. We spoke our own language and farmed the land. We made our own clothes, our own tools; whatever we needed, we made a way to survive. We paid taxes, but still the state refused to call us citizens. When the Civil War was underway, many of our people were called to fight, my grandfather included. He fought to defend the Confederacy, but when it was all over, he and the tribe were back to being Indians that the white man wanted to push as far away from him as possible. The push for us to go to Oklahoma continued as strong as ever. Some of us took to the road, others stayed to establish their homes on the reservation in North Carolina. We suffered from diseases we had never heard of before. Many of us died from the smallpox disease. That's when my grandfather took off for Virginia, taking his family with him to find a new life on the land that once belonged to our ancestors.*

21

SHORTLY AFTER nine a.m. on Monday, Kira tapped lightly on Cicely's office door. She looked through the glass panel and waited for her to beckon her inside. Her boss glanced up and nodded her in while continuing to click furiously at the keyboard, intent on finishing her thought. Cicely was tall and thin with long dark hair and dark eyes, and skin as white as copy paper. Her long fingers looked like spider legs dancing across the keys. Kira had worked with Cicely since she took over the Features department two years ago. Cicely had replaced Burt Wells, whom Kira had loved as an editor and a teacher. She didn't mind working for Cicely, but she didn't love it either. Clutching the newspaper with her buried story, she waited and grew more nervous in the silence. At last, her boss stopped typing and asked what she could do for her. Kira stumbled as she began the spiel she had practiced on her drive in. She didn't want to get a reputation as a complainer, but still, this was a legitimate complaint.

"I was wondering why my story on the Native Americans was pushed to page eleven." She displayed the page holding it up. Cicely looked at it thoughtfully for a moment, then raised her eyebrows and gazed at Kira.

"I expected it to be the main story for the section," Kira continued. "We had talked about that at our department meeting."

"Kira, I don't know. You'd have to ask whoever was on the desk on Saturday night."

Kira nodded. "Yes, but I thought we had discussed it and it was slated as the lead story. I didn't think City Desk had any authority to change that decision."

"Kira, City Desk makes final decisions all the time, especially when there's breaking news."

Kira's heart rattled heavily in her chest. No breaking news occurred that would have affected the Features section. "But, Mark's story on the old man could have run at any time. My story was more timely. It was—"

Cicely cut in, her hand raised as if to stop traffic. "I don't know what happened, okay? We managed to get it in."

Kira gave another try, but her words were stopped once again. Cicely wanted to hear nothing more. She had work to do, she said. A slap across the face would not have stung more than Cicely's dismissal. Holding in her fury, Kira turned and left the office. The brains at the top of this small-minded newspaper always got their way, she thought. As she reached her desk she saw Mark sitting on the other side of the room gesturing and talking on the phone. Like her, he had grown up in the Fort Lewis area, but unlike her, he had grown up on the affluent white side of town. She didn't like what she was feeling and walked into the newsroom where she found Beverly at her desk.

"You ready for this meeting this afternoon?" Beverly said tapping the statement the black reporters were planning to present to the managing editor criticizing the recent crime series. Kira recounted her words with Cicely and wanted to make sure the topic about how the paper treats other races also was discussed at the reporters' meeting.

Beverly shook her head. "There's gonna be trouble this afternoon. I can feel it."

THE MANAGING editor read the statement issued by the Minority Affairs Committee denouncing the portrayal of blacks in the papers' recent series on crime. Dan Barker read the statement, daintily holding the rim of his spectacles with forefinger and thumb, as if it were a notice for employees to fill out their timesheets correctly. He was a short man with a ruddy weathered complexion that reflected his childhood growing up on a farm. Kira knew he loved to garden, but he seemed too fastidious to have worked in fields or with livestock. He finished reading and removed his glasses with a flourish before looking at the gathering of news reporters, features writers, sports writers and photographers jammed into the conference room. He called for comments. The room remained silent. He pulled a pen from behind his ear and waited a moment before marking his agenda and moving on to the next topic.

"Wait a minute!" Pete rose from his seat in the middle of the room and cleared his throat. "Nobody's got a damn thing to say?"

An awkward silence followed and a few rolled their eyes, then a voice rumbled from the back. Sarcastic, asking what people were supposed to say. The voice belonged to Aaron Gant, the author of the crime series. He was a stocky man in his thirties who liked to brag about how many pounds he could bench press. He had won several prizes for his investigative pieces on local government, and management considered him a star reporter on the staff, but Kira wasn't impressed with his conceited attitude. She respected healthy competition, however, Gant's desire to step on others to always be number one had made plenty of enemies. He grew up in a small town in Missouri outside Kansas City and claimed to be on his way to *The New York Times*.

Pete said he wasn't looking for apologies, but expected a discussion on why this came about and what the paper was going do about the insult to the black community. Barker broke in saying nothing could be done now. "Your complaint has been noted."

"But sensitive stories like this shouldn't come up in a vacuum," Pete said. "There should be some discussion around it."

"What's so sensitive about people who are concerned about rising crime in their neighborhood?" Aaron asked.

Both Pete and Aaron's voices began to rise as their argument escalated. Pete contended that the crimes themselves were not the committee's issue. His concern lay in the story insinuating that only black people were committing those crimes.

"And who's to say they're not?" said Aaron.

"You!" Pete yelled. "You, as an objective journalist, shouldn't take sides."

"We take sides all the time. When we see an injustice or write about a cause, we're taking a side."

Cate stood up and joined the discussion. "That's crap," she said. "Whether we believe one thing or another, it's our job to present the whole story, not just one view of it. And it's clear in this case that this paper has only one view."

"Enough!" Barker shouted. But he couldn't stop Beverly from adding her voice to the fray, asking what was the point of the committee? Before even reading a word, the cartoon picture was insulting to blacks. Barker, flicking the agenda in front of him, tried to calm the room down, suggesting any interested parties get together to discuss the matter after the meeting. But Pete was through. He bumped his chair with the back of his knees as he stood up. The chair fell, hitting the knees of the person sitting behind him, and he stormed out. Kira looked at Beverly, who shrugged and followed Pete. The newspaper's apathy toward non-whites had never been so blatant. Although Kira had always known it existed, she felt shocked somehow. Her heart racing, she sat for a moment, wanting to explain what this meant to the black reporters and to the black community, that it wasn't the committee nitpicking the paper, that it was much more serious. The newspaper had to make a greater effort to diversify its coverage, to fully reflect the communities that it served. She hesitated then stood up. As she did, several other reporters rose and trooped out. She followed, heading back to the newsroom where she heard Pete raging. He cursed the newspaper and everyone in it. He wasn't coming back. Beverly stood nearby, her grumblings drowned out by Pete's ravings. Then Aaron showed up.

"Anything you've got to say about my work, you say it to my face," Aaron shouted across the room. "Who the hell do you think you are writing up a denouncement of something I put hours into, huh?"

"Fuck you," Pete said. "This wasn't personal, Aaron. This is something this newspaper has been doing long before you got out of diapers. You've been here, what, two, three years? Black folks are tired of seeing negative stereotypical images of themselves on the front page. We've been seeing it for decades and it's time to stop."

"Truth hurts, huh?"

The comment was said softly but not quietly enough to escape Beverly. "And what's that supposed to mean?" she asked. Aaron turned his sneer toward her and said nothing. Beverly took a step toward him, challenging him with her stare. He shook his head.

"Look, it's not my fault you people chose drug dealing and crime to make a living. The stats prove it. Y'all are aggressive and your *folks* are bringing this country down."

Pete almost flew across the room to grab Aaron by the throat. "You mothafu—" As Pete hit him, Aaron stumbled backwards into a desk and the pair hit the ground knocking over a computer screen that landed with a thud in the aisle. Surprisingly, the screen didn't break. Pete and Aaron rolled over each other grunting and groaning, arms flailing, fists pounding muscle. Kira stared in disbelief while Beverly let loose a series of shrieks and paced on the periphery of the chaos. Notebooks and pens fell to the floor as the two men scuffled. Pete staggered to his feet and lunged at Aaron as he struggled to stand. The pair slammed into the wall and just as Pete landed a right hook on Aaron's jaw, a security officer appeared and grabbed Pete in a chokehold.

The managing editor bellowed from the opposite end of the newsroom that Pete was fired and called for Aaron to come to his office. Barker stood for a moment tapping his glasses against his thigh, then departed. His announcement stopped everything.

"You've got to be kidding," Beverly said. Her face flushed burgundy; she blinked and looked from Kira to Pete who was attempting to tear himself out of the security officer's grip.

"They can't fire Pete and not fire Aaron as well," Beverly yelled.

Finally free of the officer, Pete glared at the space where Barker had stood. When Kira realized her jaw was open, she closed her mouth and swallowed a dry lump. Without a second thought she stormed after Barker, threw open his office door and stood in the frame. Aaron was leaning back in the chair with his hand over his bloody face. She stared at Barker. Since coming to the paper she had admired him. He had always appeared to be supportive of her, and she had felt comfortable approaching him with story ideas or questions. She had thought him to be sensitive to race relations and the need to make amends for the years past when the city newspaper had ignored blacks and other non-white communities, when the bridal page was filled with all white smiling faces and the crime reports came from the same black sections of town. This was not the same man she had respected.

"I don't understand," she said.

"You can't argue with the facts of the story," Aaron said.

"What about the facts you left out, like the fact that the majority of drug dealers and users in this city are white middle class. Where's that story?"

"Stop it!" Barker said. He ordered Aaron to fetch a cold compress for his nose. When the door clicked closed Kira stared at the man she thought could help the newspaper make a real shift in the city's race relations.

"Sit down, Kira."

"No, I will not sit down. I thought this newspaper was making an effort to stop this kind of insanity. Firing Pete and not Aaron is only going to cause a rift between the blacks and whites in your own newsroom. This wasn't personal between Aaron and Pete. We were objecting to the fact that blacks are portrayed all too often as criminals in the media, and we thought our job as the Minority Affairs Committee was to highlight those instances and enlighten the rest of the staff. It was an opportunity for discussion. What happened today has only heightened the tension. And it's not just blacks. What do you think the Native American community thought when they saw my story get buried in Sunday's paper, if they saw it at all? That says we don't care about their issues."

Barker leaned back in his chair and glanced at his desk. "Kira, I'm sorry that you're upset," he said, pressing his forefingers and thumbs together. "First of all, I don't have to justify my actions to you, but Pete was assaulting Aaron and that warrants dismissal. Secondly, the committee was not designed to make decisions on stories and layout. Now, why you think this picture of the African-American man was offensive, I don't know. Beverly says it's insulting. What's wrong with it? Kira, I've heard people say African Americans are way too sensitive, and to be honest this whole incident seems to prove that it's true."

"Too sensitive?" Kira closed her eyes and shook her head.

His voice softened. He would look into it, but he was convinced that no matter what the newspaper did, the African-American community would always be upset for one reason or another. "You can't please everybody."

"And you don't think we should do anything to change that?"

Barker threw his hands out in surrender. "We've hired black reporters, but they don't stay. We have a minority intern program, and we've been doing positive stories on minorities. Last week, we had that profile of the black teacher who got the Teacher of the Year award—"

Kira walked out of the office leaving the door open. Aaron stood outside pressing a wad of damp tissues over the bridge of his nose. She looked at him and said, "I hope it's broken," then returned to the newsroom. While a small group of reporters huddled in the middle of the room speculating on the fight, most of the others had either left or were back at their computers. The knocked-over computer screen had miraculously disappeared as if tidying up the mess would put everything back to normal. Kira stood shivering, chilled by what had just transpired. She saw no sign of Beverly or Pete, and spotted Patricia at Cate's desk, the pair standing in shocked silence.

"I'm sick to my stomach," Patricia said. "After fifteen years working here, this is what I'm witnessing?" Her forehead wrinkled as she shook her head. She couldn't say anything more and simply walked away.

KIRA FOUND Beverly at her mother's house and invited her out to dinner. After such a dreadful day, surely they both needed a drink. Too often they promised to spend time — dinner, lunch, drinks after work — but actions never followed their words. A year, at least, had passed since they had done anything together outside of work. Kira wanted to spend this evening with her girl-friend.

They sat opposite each other in a booth, soothed by the dim lighting, potted plants and stained glass lamps of the chain restaurant, and said little. The day's events had stunned them both. Conversation came slowly: a recounting of their shock at Pete's firing and pondering what the future would hold for him before drifting to more mundane topics, each sharing a brief update on their mothers, and Beverly providing a glowing report on Tamika's efforts in first grade. Beverly asked about Jamal and Kira began to respond with the usual, *He's fine. We're fine. All is fine.* But she stopped herself. All was not fine and she needed to talk to someone.

"It's an empty relationship. I don't think I can be with him anymore," Kira said, her words as much a surprise to herself as to Beverly.

"I thought you were happy with him."

"We've had some fun times, but something's missing."

"At least you have someone."

Kira wasn't sure how to respond. She didn't want to resurrect old resentments and have Beverly perceive her as being self-righteous, yet she wanted to be honest. "I'd rather be alone than have someone who isn't right for me."

Beverly began listing her choices for dinner from the menu. So much rattled inside Kira that she wanted to share — her confusion about her father, about Alex, about Jamal, about leaving Fort Lewis for good. The day's events had solidified her desire to leave. But Beverly had slammed the door closed, and Kira didn't have the strength to push it open again.

22

A LEX ENJOYED sex in the morning, still half asleep, reaching beside him to feel the soft skin of a woman, the firmness of her thighs, her hips, the sound of her sigh, the smell of her skin, her kisses, all creating a rush of blood through his body, his pulse rising until his mind leaped over the edge into quiet oblivion, an intense meditation that prepared him for the day ahead. Except each morning that Lorett had awakened beside him, she had destroyed that precious moment of acute silence when his brain bathed in each sensation slowly fading from his body. Clearly, with Lorett, sex was better at night when she would fall asleep afterwards. Lying naked beside him, she chattered on and on about the wedding, competing with the chatter of the birds in the tree outside the window. He watched the cotton-ball clouds drift across the sky while she talked about colors and flowers and invitations and dresses and bridesmaids, and they would write their own vows and she would sing and he would dance. The ceremony would incorporate some Indian traditions, but she wanted a white gown with a tiara and a long train. She wanted to look like a princess and—

"Shut up!"

He didn't mean to say the words aloud, but they slipped out, loud enough for her to hear. Her face was stricken, and for a moment he was sorry until she began again, her voice rising in frustration at his disinterest in their future. He was supposed to be planning the event *with* her — the most important day of their lives — it had to be perfect, and wouldn't be unless he put forth some effort, and on and on. She sat up on her knees, holding the sheet over her chest.

"Jesus Christ, Alex, what the fuck is wrong with you? First you don't show up at our Blessing Ceremony — how the hell you could forget something like that I'll never know. I'm seriously getting the impression you don't want to get married at all. But you promised me, remember?"

He raised his palms to her, as if he could deflect her voice, or better still, silence her but she ignored him and continued to rant. "Why aren't we married already? Don't you love me?" Those words she had said countless times the last few days. Didn't he love her?

"This is not just my wedding, Alex. It's *our* wedding."

"Fine. Write down what you want me to do, and I'll do it," he said.

That wasn't good enough. She wanted his enthusiasm, his active participation and involvement in the planning. He should be making decisions, too. He, however, wanted her and her mother to plan it, to do everything necessary so that all he had to do was show up, wearing whatever they said he should wear. He would say, "I do" and it would be over. He covered his face with his hands and groaned. She slapped his shoulder then got out of the bed, snatched her clothes from the floor and briskly got dressed. "Fine then."

"Fine."

"Fine," she said again and left with her sandals snapping against the stairs. He heard the blinds on the back door clatter as it opened and shut. Feeling the tension gnaw his shoulders, Alex pressed the back of his head into the pillow. He tried to empty his thoughts but images of constant arguments between himself and Lorett crammed his head. He didn't want to get married if it meant daily bickering, if it meant feeling guilty because he wasn't meeting his wife's expectations.

The door downstairs squeaked open as his father came in. They had barely spoken since the attack as Alex thought of it. Should he tell his father he couldn't stay, couldn't go through with the wedding? Perhaps forgetting about the ceremony had been no accident? Perhaps unconsciously he had put it out of his mind? In his heart, he knew he didn't want to get married. He would have to leave. To hell with heredity and tradition. Alex felt certain he was not the right man for the job. He didn't want to live the same life as his father. He didn't want to watch his wife grow weary and depressed while he struggled to be faithful. Watch her wither until she couldn't stand it anymore and end her life with a rope like his mother.

His father called to him to get downstairs. The store didn't open till ten, but each morning his father liked to go over the books and inventory before opening the doors, and Alex was supposed to help. He hated taking care of the books.

When he finally joined his father in the store, he felt the urge to ask about his mother, but the air was already tense between them. Raising the subject would make matters worse. Richard set a tray of bills on the counter and pulled out the checkbook from the cabinet below. Alex took a cloth from under the counter and began dusting the display cases and trinkets. They had never talked about his mother; the topic never came up. Today he would force his father to talk about her. For years, he had tiptoed around his father's emotions and the question that had danced in his mind for so long suddenly pirouetted off his tongue.

"Why did you marry Mom?"

Richard's fluid writing motion paused and his hand hovered over the checkbook. His eyes closed for a moment then he looked at Alex. "Because she was beautiful, and she played softball to win."

"Honestly."

Richard looked at Alex for a moment then lowered his eyes and stared at the paperwork before him. "Why are you asking this?"

"I want to know."

"Her father was the chief of the Wolf Clan. He thought it would be good for the tribe for us to marry, bringing the strongest families in the Wolf and the Bird clans together. It wasn't one of those arranged marriages, though. If we'd protested, I don't think anyone would have forced us. But our families were strong leaders. The children were expected to lead."

"Did you love her? I mean, really love her?"

"Of course I loved her. I loved her more than the earth."

"But she wasn't happy."

"Alex, I can't talk about this," Richard said turning to walk away. Alex caught his arm.

"Paw, please. I have to understand what happened."

Alex followed his father into the office where Richard filled a glass with water from the small sink. Gulping, he emptied the glass. He returned to the counter and stood staring at the floor, clenching his fists. Quietly, he began to talk about his marriage never once looking at Alex.

Mary and Richard had gladly married, but struggled in those early years when he was studying at the university. He had graduated with a business degree and went on to get his juris doctorate. Mary complained of his lack of interest in her and flaunted her promiscuity, although he never showed how much it hurt him. She taunted him with the names of men she had met at the mall or at the nightclub, but he felt helpless to change the path she had chosen. They fought bitterly until she finally walked out on him after two years of marriage. Some months passed before she returned five months pregnant. At first, Richard wasn't sure it was his child, but he couldn't turn her away. They tried again, settling down together and working hard to make a good life for their baby Andrew, whose features undoubtedly revealed he was Richard's son. She got a part-time job as a receptionist in the small law office in Fort Lewis where Richard worked as a junior attorney. Eventually, he opened his own real estate law firm above the gift shop. For a while, Mary continued her job at the law office and helped Richard manage his books until the business grew enough for her to work full-time with him. While Richard lost himself in his work, Mary grew frustrated with the monotony of her life, and the lack of help from her husband in caring for their toddler. When she became pregnant again, she quit her job and took up quilting. He needed office help and hired Ruthann Kelmer as his assistant.

Richard fell silent. Alex stared at his father wanting to know why his mother had hanged herself. He and Andrew had asked the question several times after her funeral, with little response from their father until he finally said, "We don't know, so don't bother asking no more. She's gone and that's it." Until now, Alex had never had the courage to ask again, and with the thought fresh in his mind, the question got stuck in his throat.

In quiet moments alone, he could still smell her death. He was seven. The day had been bright and cold; winter had settled in. Maw was nowhere around, not in the kitchen where he expected her to be cooking dinner; no food simmered on the stove and he was hungry. Andy was playing with his friend down the street. Snow was in the air and Alex wanted to catch the first flakes. He stepped into the screened-in porch to find Muskey — they would play with the bouncy ball in the back yard. As he stepped across the threshold calling for the dog, a stench of what he thought was dog poop stung his nose. Then he saw her legs dangling from the wooden beam at the far end of the porch, a mile away in his memory. The stool Paw sat on when he was carving had been toppled over. Alex walked across the expanse, sensing something wrong. When he finally reached the stool, he set it upright for her to step down. Her brown skirt hung stiffly around her legs and a run in her stockings crept along her calf. The wind blew through the trees and blustered into the porch, yet her body remained motionless, the rope, thin and gray, reaching down from the ceiling, disappeared into her collar. She never stepped down. She never answered him as he stood there calling her, screaming for her to wake up and start dinner.

Now, he watched his father pick up the pen and gaze blankly at the open checkbook. Resentment swelled in his chest. At the time, he had been too young to understand what had happened, but Andrew told him their father had been with Ruthann when he should have been with their mother.

"I can't marry Lorett," he said.

Richard slowly raised his head to look at him but said nothing.

"I can't," Alex repeated.

"Don't be foolish."

"I'm not ready. She wouldn't be happy with me. You said it yourself. I'm selfish and irresponsible."

His father's grasp on the pen tightened. "Here are the invoices that are due. You write the checks," Richard said. He set the pen firmly on the counter, walked around his son and left the shop out the front door. Alex felt caught by the snare of his father's desire that he continue the Harper line and didn't know how to wriggle his way out. Although he wanted to, he couldn't go back to Gloria in New Mexico. He missed her more than he had thought he would. Living with her forever had never been a possibility, marriage had never been a consideration, yet being without her had left an emptiness that surprised him. She had nurtured his art and refined his skill, mothered and protected him, loved him. Her world had allowed him to test new-found wings, explore fresh skies, soar, stumble, and rise again. In her eyes, he stood in no-one's shadow. His family didn't exist — he didn't have to think about his brother, his mother or his father's expectations. If he crashed, Gloria dusted him off to try again. She had faith in his art, pushing him past boundaries he put upon himself. With her guidance, he won three local competitions and sold his work in two large exhibits. In her arms, he knew there was nothing he couldn't try. He had loved her without strings . . . without obligation . . . without fear.

～

THE GREEN velvet deepened her skin tone and her shoulders seemed to glow under her bedroom lamp. Kira hadn't seen or heard from Jamal in several days, but he had called this afternoon, asking her out to a dinner party. She had politely declined, but he insisted. He showed up at her door expecting her to be ready. When he saw that she wasn't, he demanded she get dressed immediately.

"Goddamn you, Jamal. I said I'm tired and I am *not* going."

He frowned at her like a frustrated father with his defiant toddler. "Woman, don't you curse me."

She closed her eyes as he leaned into her face, his warm breath slapping her cheeks. "Now get your ass in something sexy and let's go. I ain't got time to play your stupid game right now. I got clients expecting me to be there on time."

She took a deep breath and looked at him, wanting to refuse. Giving in was easier than continuing the battle. For too long, she had hidden behind masks she created to suit the situation. As a journalist she could pry into people's lives, ask questions she wouldn't dare to ask in any other position. Her notebook and pen gave her license to walk into situations she would normally never enter. As Jamal's woman she could be the sensuous seductress, wield her sexuality without any incrimination. She played the role of the responsible, good daughter for her mother, staying by her side in times of need.

Journalist, lover, daughter, and now she had a white father. Who was she inside? What color was her soul?

Slipping her painted toenails into dark green suede pumps, she pivoted in front of the full-length mirror. Jamal wanted to see this side of her. What would Alex think of her now, all dressed up. Jamal expected her to wear sexy clothes — a person's appearance was most important to him. He would never be seen dead in a pair of scruffy cowboy boots. Kira laughed at the thought. After eighteen months of playing seductress with Jamal, she didn't find their games so fulfilling. She sprayed herself with perfume and descended the stairs.

"I'm tempted to forget about dinner and go straight for dessert," he said.

"Choice is yours." Kira pulled away from him and straightened her dress. "But I am hungry."

"Me too." He raised an eyebrow at her.

"I mean for food."

Jamal snickered. A bottle of brandy and two glasses already sat on the dining table. Kira re-filled her own glass and handed the other to Jamal who made a great display of taking a sip. She watched him sitting on the edge of her couch wearing a dark gray suit, his legs crossed, changing channels. She didn't want this anymore.

As they drove to the restaurant, Kira half listened to him ramble on about his boss not allowing him to take the lead on a new project. Her thoughts were jumbled.

"What do you think of interracial relationships?" she asked when Jamal was finally quiet.

"I can go for blacks mixing with Latinos, and maybe Asians, but not white. That's a no-no. I can't go there."

"Why?"

He contemplated her for a moment before asking why she needed to know. Kira shrugged. "Maybe it's 'cause of our history," he said. "Maybe 'cause I don't think a white woman would ever fully understand me. I don't know for sure, but it ain't something I'm interested in."

"So you'd be against any black person dating a Caucasian?"

Stopped at a red light, Jamal turned to look at her. "You seeing a white guy?"

Kira laughed. "I'm just curious to see what you think."

"I ain't gonna call them names or nothing like that if I see a mixed couple on the street together, but I ain't gonna respect the brotha or sistah who's with a white person. It ain't right. But that's just me."

"What about a child from a mixed relationship? What would you think of that?"

"I wouldn't dis a child cause one of his parents was white." He paused. "Is this a story you're working on for the newspaper?"

Kira nodded vigorously. "Yeah, it might be a story. I'm just getting some ideas."

What would Jamal think of her father being white? Maybe it wasn't important what he thought. Maybe she didn't want to hear anything else he had to say about anything.

THE RESTAURANT was open for the private party only and filled with a select group of business clients. Along the sidewall chefs in white prepared an assortment of dishes for an extravagant buffet. She tasted the stir-fry shrimp and some of the roast beef — all delicious. While Jamal schmoozed, Kira smiled graciously when introduced and said little. She found a spot at the bar and knocked back two more glasses of wine while watching Jamal make his rounds. He nodded toward a young man at the other end of the bar, expecting her to start the game, to flirt and tease this man until Jamal retrieved her for himself. Tonight, though, she didn't feel like playing and wondered how she had fallen into such a miserable relationship, with little depth or meaning. Her life as a whole seemed meaningless. Looking around the room she counted seven black people out of a crowd of roughly seventy-five, not including the wait staff. She had to get away from Fort Lewis and go somewhere more diverse with more social and professional opportunities, and where she could meet more appealing men interested in more than just her body. She caught herself about to order another glass of wine and felt instantly cheerless. She ordered a club soda instead. Soon, she would be thirty with nothing to show for her life — not a husband and family, not a fulfilling career with a chance to advance, nothing but a string of empty relationships and a job that faked its concern for the growing non-white communities.

Kira stumbled as she stood and began walking between the tables to the exit. She heard Jamal call her name but kept moving. She rummaged through her purse to tip the coat-check attendant and saw rain was drizzling outside. Jamal grabbed her arm and swung her around insisting that she stay, but she jerked away from him. "Not this time," she said, and almost ran out the door. The restaurant was located on a side street and she would have to walk down a slight hill to the main road to get a taxi. Walking in high heels in the rain wasn't appealing. And who knows how long it would take to get a cab.

23

THE MAIN section of the community center had been erected in the mid 1800s. The brick building was two levels high with eight tall gaping windows that Alex always imagined as the black eyes of a spider. On the rear, a large wooden hall had been added around 1950. Three years ago, Alex joined his father and other men to install vinyl siding, purchased with funds raised by the community. Although already late for the meeting, he paused to look at the trim around the entrance. The vinyl made the building always look freshly painted.

Inside, people crowded the place. In the main hall, he heard his grandfather's voice reviewing the account balance and recounting his meeting earlier in the week with Mrs. Foster. She was willing to give them more time to raise funds, but wanted to be rid of her land by the fall. And if that meant selling to the Parks Department, so be it.

PawPaw looked tired. Alex could tell the old man had lost weight in recent months and it worried him. He had slowed down considerably, too, and wasn't as vibrant as Alex had come to expect. After his mother's death, Alex's grandparents had raised him and Andy. While the boys lived with their father in the house down the hill from their grandparents, they had spent most of their time following PawPaw around his backyard and traipsing after him to the store where he taught them how to carve wood — how to work the hardwoods versus the softwoods, oak versus pine, maple versus spruce. He taught them how to bow hunt for deer.

Andy had teased Alex for not being able to shoot the bow straight. He had gotten queasy watching MawMaw clean the hide but didn't tell anyone for fear Andy would tease him about that as well. In the Cherokee tradition, PawPaw had given his grandsons their Indian names: Alex was Quiet Hawk, and Andy was Strong Foot. Those names had almost been forgotten as the boys had grown, choosing to use the Anglo-Saxon names given by their mother.

As a youngster, Alex so wanted to be like his big brother, except when Andy cut his hair short the year he entered middle school. Alex mimicked almost everything his brother did, but took a stand against cutting his hair, preferring to keep it long like Paw and PawPaw. When Andy fell ill with bronchitis, Alex pretended to be sick, too. He sat on his brother's bed coughing every time Andy coughed, and running on command to fetch whatever his brother asked of him. He even stole Paw's *Hustler* magazines from the back of his closet for Andy, who had apparently found them months earlier when searching for Paw's penknife. At least that's what he had said at the time. Now, Alex wasn't so sure his brother had been telling the truth, though back then he had believed every word. When the bronchitis developed into pneumonia and Andy was taken to the hospital, Alex slept in his brother's bed in the room they shared above the kitchen. Four nights later, PawPaw had sat with Alex on the bed and gently told him his brother had passed away. Alex was twelve. He knew what death meant. He knew his brother was now with their mother. Yet he kept asking, "What do you mean he's dead? How can he be dead?" Pneumonia was just a bad cold. It wasn't supposed to kill anyone. PawPaw had held his grandson tightly for hours as Alex had sobbed. Alex hadn't known then that downstairs his grandmother was comforting his father in much the same way.

Now, in the community center, his father sat on one side of PawPaw at the head table and MawMaw sat on the other side. Four-foot long tables had been set end to end, making a large rectangle where the Committee of Clans sat. Metal folding chairs encircled the committee and were filled with citizens from the community. He spotted Lorett sitting with her mother along the back wall. He returned her wave with a nod. Because no more seats were available, he leaned against the wall next to the door. His father's look toward him clearly said, "Couldn't you have gotten here on time?" Alex simply looked away, sliding his hands into his pockets. He tried to listen attentively to the discussion; people were suggesting ways to raise more funds: bake sales, letter-writing campaigns, another powwow.

Amid the hum of the ceiling fans and the voices, Alex's mind strayed. He wondered what Kira would think of this meeting and if she would want to follow-up with another story in the paper. He would suggest to his father that he could contact the paper and push for another story; perhaps take on a more active role with PR. It would be a good opportunity to show his father he was capable and willing to work for the community, and an excuse to call the reporter. He liked Kira. Her mind was sharp and witty, and she was sexy too, the way her hips swayed when she walked. Her body was firm and soft in all the right places. Kira reminded him of Gloria, although his professor was much older. But they had the same dark eyes and both frowned when they were mulling something over. Both were resolute and opinionated, they didn't look for men to take care of them. He found that appealing in a woman. He rarely considered race or color. He was more interested in the shape of their minds, and their bodies.

Lorett had been strong-willed when she was younger. Still sassy, but now, she expected him to take charge of everything. She had sat him down last evening to talk about their problems and he listened while she listed all the things he was doing wrong: he didn't hold her enough, he didn't tell her he loved her enough, he didn't talk to her about his feelings, he wasn't spending enough time with her and spent too much time making sculptures or drinking with his friends, he never wanted to do anything fun. Alex clenched his teeth and said nothing. When was the last time *she* had initiated something fun? He was tired of having to fulfill her needs. She wanted him to buy her things, to take her out to parties and nightclubs, to movies, to sit with her and plan the wedding, to be there whenever she needed him, which was constantly. He didn't find any of that fun. When she finally stopped talking, he was so overwhelmed he couldn't respond.

"Well, say something."

"What the hell am I supposed to say to all that?"

"What are you going to do about it?"

"Lorett, I don't think there's anything I can say or do that will make you happy." He left her alone in her mother's sitting room. He didn't understand why his proposal and intent to marry her wasn't enough — yes, he had messed up, but he was trying to make things better; he just didn't want to turn into somebody else to make everyone else happy.

As the meeting ended and everyone headed out, he saw Lorett with her mother a few steps behind, making a straight line for him. At the same time, he saw his father approaching. He was in no mood for either of them. Lorett greeted him with a quick kiss on his lips and grabbed his hand. He leaned forward and kissed her mother's cheek. Behind her stood his father.

"Alex, if you're going to bother showing up, the least you can do is come to these meetings on time."

"I'm sorry, I—"

"You should be taking more responsibility. I can't do everything."

Alex looked uncomfortably from Lorett to her mother, who squeezed Alex's hand and said he was welcome to stop in at her house anytime. She gave Richard a stern look as she said goodnight. Lorett walked her mother to the car then came back into the hall.

"Paw, I'm not ready for all this."

"Then get ready." Richard shook his head. "Christ, Alex, when are you ever gonna be ready for anything? When are you ever gonna start living the life you're supposed to be living." Richard stomped away. Alex unclenched his fists and closed his eyes struggling to calm his breathing. He felt Lorett's hand on his arm and fought the urge to push her away. She suggested they take a vacation, spend a couple of days just the two of them in Florida, somewhere with a beach. Alex kept silent. The last thing he wanted was to be confined somewhere with her. He watched his father on the other side of the hall talking with PawPaw and wondered if they were discussing his ineptitude. Lorett rubbed his arm and asked what was wrong. After a pause he said, "I need some time."

Her voice switched from gentle to harsh. "Time for what?"

"Just some time, Lorett. Please?"

She shook her head, looking past him, her lips pursed, and he knew what she was thinking. Hadn't he said the same words before leaving for New Mexico? Hadn't he told her he wanted to get married, but just not yet? He had felt those same pressures then to become someone he knew he wasn't. A husband. A father. A community leader. None appeared to fit. And if he had to hear Ms. Wilson ask one more time if MawMaw was making Lorett's wedding dress, he was going to dive head first into Deer Creek. He didn't have what it took to be a take-charge organizer who would solve everyone's problems. He wasn't like his brother, who always knew how to make things right. Alex was the boy who had stood in Andy's shadow, who couldn't shoot straight, couldn't hit a baseball, clammed up when he had to give an oral report in school, drew pictures instead of writing essays, a C student who daydreamed his way through high school.

Alex was deeply sorry for disappointing Lorett yet again but knew the words wouldn't satisfy her. He wasn't ready to step into the box everyone seemed to have open for him and he couldn't stop himself from running away again. Without a word, Lorett turned and walked out of the building. Alex watched her go and stared out the door into the dark. Rain pattered on the grass. As he stood there, he felt a familiar presence behind him.

"PawPaw, when will I ever be enough?"

His grandfather moved forward into his view. "You've always been a handful, Alex."

"You know what I mean. When will people accept me for who I am?"

"When *you* figure out who you are and accept yourself."

～

SHE KEPT walking, following the wet street and wondering if a taxi would ever appear. A truck pulled up next to her and she cringed. Clasping her purse closer to her chest, she walked as fast as she could in heels along a damp sidewalk. A voice called out to her and she kept moving, afraid. "Don't I know you?" A cheap line she was not going to fall for. Praying for a cab, she looked up and down the street. "Kira, right?" Hearing her name stopped her and she looked at the driver. Alex Harper.

Seated at a corner table in a nearby bar she explained why she was wandering the streets alone, escaping from a relationship she couldn't justify anymore. He explained that he, too, was escaping from a relationship — relationships — from a woman and his family.

She didn't understand. From where she sat, he had the perfect life — a woman who loved him, a strong family unit and a family business focused around his culture. He ran the side of his forefinger up and down his glass, smearing the condensation and keeping quiet. She asked if she had said something wrong, still he said nothing. The clink and crash of the bar rose around them. Alex leaned forward, wrapping his fingers firmly around his beer.

"I know this guy, someone I went to high-school with, he's serving time for selling drugs, amphetamines, I think. My father says he didn't have enough respect for himself and his culture. Then there's me. I've been fed the teachings and traditions since I was born, to make me strong and proud. But I feel pressure to be something I'm not. There has to be a place between me and the guy in prison."

"So how do you get there?"

He shrugged. "We're not as cohesive as you might think. Maybe getting the land back will help us all. My grandfather has spent all his life trying to maintain the importance of the tribe and its clans."

"Don't you think that's important?"

"Have you ever felt like you're not where you're supposed to be? That maybe you're not who you thought you were? Does that even make sense?"

His words made complete sense. Kira thought of her features — her round nose and flared nostrils, her round full lips. She had never thought of herself as anything less than a proud African-American woman. While her skin was café-au-lait, it never dawned on her that she was actually half and half. She had looked into the blue eyes of a man who said he was her father and she had seen only a hint of herself. Was her face a proud blending of the races, or was it the shameful face of a bastard produced from a lustful mistake?

She listened to Alex talk about himself, about more than his ancestry, more than she had heard in the interview with his father and grandfather. He spoke about his mother, about his brother. With his story on the table, she felt the desire to share with him her own story. For so long she had maintained an air of mystery around men, rarely talking about her family or anything she considered too personal. She slept with them and left it at that. But with Alex, she wanted to tell, wanted to share what little she knew of who she was.

"All these years I thought my father was dead. I met him recently for the first time. We had coffee. It was . . . eerie, like a dream. I sat across from him not believing he was my father, yet knowing it was true. I always knew my brother's father wasn't my dad. I don't think anyone ever said anything about it. I used to imagine I was the daughter of some diplomat killed overseas or a king or someone exotic." She chuckled. "As it turned out he's some truck driver who's been afraid to face his daughter for the last twenty-nine years."

He wanted to know why the man had appeared in her life now, but Kira couldn't answer his question. Instead, she asked him, "How do you feel about your mother's death?"

"It was a long time ago. I was real little, but sometimes I still feel angry at her. And I feel sorry for her. I don't know what she went through, what she felt. Why she couldn't find a way to be happy."

"If you could speak to her again, what would you say?"

"I'd want to know what my father could have done to make her happy, to make her want to continue living. But I can't change anything now. It's done. Like with your father. You can't change his color even if you want to, or change his reason for leaving your mom. You just accept it."

"Sometimes I think I hate him, but I don't really know what I feel. Maybe it would be good to get to know him."

"Maybe it's not him you hate. Maybe it's that you didn't know the truth. Besides, what could it hurt to talk to him?"

He reached across the table and stroked the back of her hand. His eyes were gentle, shadowed by the soft lights of the bar, soft lips framed crooked white teeth. Slowly he leaned back, away from her, letting his fingers slide down her hand to the tips of her nails before reaching for his drink.

They stayed in the bar drinking and talking until Alex announced he should take her home while he could still drive. In the truck, she gave him her address and directions. The music in the tape deck was Native music. Kira turned up the volume, closed her eyes and listened to the voices flowing with the flute and the pounding drums. Alex sang along, his voice low and melodic making sounds more than actual words that she could understand. She remembered his dancing and suddenly felt the urge to jump and spin to the music. As if he could see her thoughts, he said he would teach her to dance, but she refused — immediately embarrassed and afraid of making a fool of herself. But he insisted. He would teach her right now! Kira laughed at his exuberance but again shook her head, yet knowing there was nothing she could say to stop him. He parked the truck, grabbed the tape and shocked Kira by hoisting her over his shoulder. Dizzy with his enthusiasm, she screamed and laughed, covering her mouth for fear of disturbing her neighbors at this early morning hour.

In a flash, they were inside, his boots and her heels discarded, the earthy music filling her home. He grabbed her hands and moved slowly, tapping his feet on her carpet. Thankful only a low side lamp illuminated her movements, she tried to follow. He released her and bounded around the room as the drums quickened, and then back, his hands at her waist spinning her around.

"Heya, hey-hey, heya…" he sang, moving close and around her. As he shifted away, she closed her eyes and bounced on her toes, feeling the rhythm. She sang, quietly at first then louder: "Heya, hey, heya, hey-hey…" Gradually, she lifted her hands above her head and skipped forward, round and round, unconstrained, free. All of a sudden, her feet flew off the carpet as Alex spun her upward and around they went, bobbing and singing.

Breathless, the pair fell to the floor, the heavy drums gone and the lilting flute now soft and haunting in the air. Kira covered her face with her hands, mortified as Alex observed her. Gently, he pulled her hands away.

"It's the best feeling in the world," he said. Kira smiled and touched his unruly hair, gingerly at first and then let her palm stroke it to the ends. She took a handful and rested it over her fingers; the strands smooth like warm milk. In turn, he reached his hand to her head and coiled her short curls around his fingertips. She sidled closer and kissed his mouth. His lips were strange, stringy in their thinness yet they pulled her into him. His hand cupped the back of her head forcing her closer. Her entire being — flushed from the dance — relished every touch from his hands as they tugged at her dress to the pressure of his mouth on her shoulders. Little by little, she led him upstairs to her bed where his body, a slightly lighter brown than her own, smothered her into the crumpled sheets. They moved together like waves caressing a deserted beach, a gentle rhythm washing over the sand until daylight changed the tide. As the sun pushed its way under the blinds and streaked across the carpet, Alex kissed Kira's lips and disappeared without a word. She lay on her side, her head resting in the hook of her arm, and watched the strip of sunshine broaden, turning the drab brown carpeting to gold.

24

KIRA DROVE the four hours south to Raleigh with her mother to visit Aunt Mae who lay prostrate on her queen-sized bed. While Kira had wanted to surprise her aunt, Martha had insisted on calling to give notice — Mae would want to make sure Buster got the bathrooms cleaned and fresh sheets on the guest-room bed.

"I know my sister, and she doesn't like those kinds of surprises. A gift maybe, but not an unexpected visit." Martha talked about the weather and the ladies at the center. Kira tried to listen but her thoughts drifted. Her mind sung with the memory of the music, of dancing, of Alex's naked body in the darkness of her bedroom. She wanted to gush about him, the way a teenager might chatter endlessly about a severe crush, but Kira was afraid to make anything more of it. More than likely, she would never see him again. This visit to Raleigh would clear her mind of everything.

Mae lived in a two-story brick house on a quaint lane in the suburbs. Tall sycamore and pine trees leaned protectively over the homes, while elderly black gentlemen fussed with the sprinkler system and brown-skinned ladies wearing straw hats trimmed the hedges.

Martha and Kira arrived before noon. Mae wanted to get up but Buster told Martha that the pain wasn't as bad when she remained flat, so Martha and Kira sat with Mae on her forget-me-not quilt and served her lemonade. They had stopped on the side of the road, unable to resist the handwritten sign announcing a peach stand up ahead. The peaches were large and juicy, so they bought a dozen.

"Fruit doesn't taste any better than what you can buy straight from the farm," Martha exclaimed. Kira had heard her mother make this claim so many times that Kira was absolutely convinced. After all, Martha's mother had been born on a farm, making Martha an authority. In Mae's spacious kitchen, Kira washed and cut the fruit and brought the plate to Mae's bedside, although Kira ate more than she gave to her aunt. Once the pile of peaches was gone, Kira gave her aunt a manicure, painting her nails bright pink, while Martha picked out her sister's silver Afro. Mae appreciated the company and Buster, thankful for the break, left to spend the afternoon wandering through the super-sized home improvement store.

"I am so fed up of laying in this bed," Mae complained. "It's been two weeks and I'm still in pain."

"Shouldn't you be in the hospital?" Kira asked.

"Peugh! The hospital? I'd be dead by now if I'd spent even a week there." She daintily scratched her nose, careful not to smudge the polish, then raised her arm for Kira to slip on three silver bangles that tinkled as they slid toward her elbow. "Tell me something interesting that's been going on in your lives."

"Hmm, let's see," Kira said. "Well, there's been an uprising at my job and I find out my father is alive and wants to get to know me. How's that for interesting?"

Not until the words were out of her mouth did Kira realize what she had said. For a split second it seemed the air disappeared from the room and outside the birds stopped chirping. Even the whir of the ceiling fan vanished. Kira braced herself for the fallout and wondered if Larry Walsh had been an issue rotting between her mother and aunt for all those years. Would her mother feel comfortable talking about it with her sister? Mae gazed at her, then looked at Martha then back at Kira. "Your father?"

Kira launched into the story about Pete getting fired at the newspaper and how Patricia had decided to take a leave of absence. She glanced at her mother who appeared thoughtful and not the least bit ruffled by the revelation. Mae, however, wasn't distracted by Kira's newspaper story.

"Did you say your father wants to get to know you?" Mae asked.

No one said a word until Mae began to rise. Martha protested, telling her to lie back down. Kira began collecting the glasses and offered to get more lemonade.

"Ya'll better stop ignoring me. Is Larry back?"

Kira finally faced her aunt's stunned expression and nodded.

"Yes, it's true," said Martha. "I was going to tell you, but I didn't know how to begin. He called a couple of weeks ago asking about Kira."

"You spoke to him?" Again, Mae started to rise but winced as she rested on her elbow.

"Lay back down, Sis," Martha said, patting Mae's shoulder. "We talked briefly. I thought it was some kind of joke at first. Then when I realized it really was him, I didn't know what to say."

"Did you talk to him, Kira?"

Now, Kira wasn't sure she wanted to talk about her meeting with Larry Walsh, but she was curious to get her aunt's opinion on the man. "I met with him."

Mae's eyes widened. "And?"

The heat in the room suddenly expanded and if the window hadn't already been open Kira would have pushed it out of its frame. She inhaled what little air was left.

"I need some water." Kira took the empty glasses downstairs to the kitchen and laid them in the sink. She let the faucet run before filling her glass then stood, staring into the back yard and sipping the luke-warm water. She gathered her muddled thoughts and took the glasses back up to Mae's room. She stood in the doorway wondering where to begin. Both her mother and aunt watched her expectedly.

"I don't know what to think about him," Kira said, taking her place on the bed. "Meeting him was strange. All these years I'd believed he was dead, and there he sat this, white man, right in front of me. I'm not sure what I'm supposed to feel or what to do."

Mae looked at her sister. "See Sister, I told you to tell her about him from the beginning."

Martha closed her eyes. "Please don't do this. I know I made a mistake, but it never, not once, occurred to me that he would come back all these years later?"

"That's why you should have told her. You never know these things. It's always best to be upfront from the start."

"Is that why you called him to tell him I'd had his child?"

Kira raised both her hands. "Stop! Don't argue. This is hard enough. It's confusing."

Mae squeezed her hand.

"Aunt Mae, tell me what you knew of him."

Her aunt stared at the ceiling for a while. "I had met him a couple times before Martha even knew him." She looked at her sister, whose head was turned toward the window. "His father taught piano in his home. He was a high-school teacher. Music, I guess. I never asked. They seemed like nice folks. My friend, Clarissa, she took lessons from him. Larry had a brother, I think, and an older sister, older than me." She shifted in the bed. "Nice people."

Kira struggled to imagine the man she had met in the diner as a teenager whose father taught the piano. It couldn't possibly be the same person.

"He drives a truck now," she said.

"A truck driver? Well, I never. I figured he'd turn out to be something more … professional."

Once again the air tightened as Mae and Martha appeared locked in a mental battle. What had transpired between these two women all those years ago? "What?" Kira asked. "What are you both thinking?"

Mae shook her head and turned her stare once again toward the ceiling. Martha looked at Kira. "Your aunt was wondering what would have happened if I had given him a chance."

"Now Sister, that was not what I was thinking."

"You know you were, 'cause I was thinking it too." Martha fell silent and began picking hair out of the comb as if it were of great importance to have the comb clean. Kira saw a deep hurt in her mother's face she had never seen before and it startled her.

"God dammit, help me up!" Mae barked.

Martha stood up and took a step back from the bed clutching the comb to her breast. "Mae, you stay exactly where you are. I'm fine. You're gonna hurt yourself."

"You're not fine. Kira, help me up outta this bed."

The energy in the room stiffened. Something was happening between her mother and aunt that Kira didn't understand, something rooted in the past, but she wasn't about to disobey her Aunt Mae. Once that woman got aggravated, it was best to do whatever she said. Kira slid her hands under her aunt's shoulders and raised her into a sitting position, all while Mae let loose a string of obscenities. Mae gestured to her sister, who acquiesced and sat down like a little girl next to her mother. Mae wrapped her arms clumsily around Martha's shoulders and patted her arm. Martha began to sob, quietly at first then it grew into a moan and Mae's grip tightened. Martha began to talk but the words were muffled into her sister's neck.

Kira was astonished. She had never seen her mother's strong spirit dissolve into tears. Until now, it had never occurred to Kira that her mother would be emotionally distressed by Larry Walsh's reappearance. She had been so focused on her own emotional turmoil that her mother's feelings had never entered her mind. Kira's stomach sank with guilt. Mae, the older of the two, the free spirit who had said having children would slow her down, now instinctively played the role of mother to her baby sister. She gestured to Kira to get the box of tissues from the side table.

"Ma, I'm so sorry," Kira said.

Her mother straightened and opened her arms to Kira. "Sweetheart, don't be sorry. I'm the one who messed everything up."

Mae and Kira both protested that Martha hadn't made a mess of anything.

"I did care about him," Martha said, dabbing a wad of tissues to her cheeks. "It wasn't that I didn't want him in our lives. It just seemed better all round to leave it alone. He was white, and Daddy was so angry."

"You let Daddy rule you," Mae said. "He shouldn't have treated you so badly, God rest his soul."

"I didn't want him to think I was a bad person. I wanted him to respect me."

Mae rolled her eyes upward. "Our daddy, the Reverend, thought everyone was bad. The problem was that you thought *you* were a bad person too, and blamed yourself for everything that didn't go right. And now with Larry coming back, you're having to deal with feelings you never took the time to resolve."

Martha squinted at her sister. "You been watching 'Oprah' again?"

All three laughed and hugged each other. Mae leaned back into the cushions and groaned. "Where's the ibuprofen?"

Kira watched her mother and aunt as they talked about their obstinate father, who refused to speak to Mae for years after she eloped. The two impersonated him and laughed and reminisced about their childhood. Kira had seen her mother vulnerable and scared when she had spent days in the hospital after suffering a heart attack. But for the first time, she saw her mother as a woman, a woman who had experienced hurt, had felt the pain of a father's criticism, and had once been in love. She began to understand why her mother had closed herself from ever loving again.

25

MARTHA FELT sick to her stomach with nerves. She moved through the kitchen wiping countertops and cabinet doors with a damp cloth. What had possessed her to call him and invite him over she couldn't fathom, but either an angel or a devil had whispered in her ear, urging her to make contact with Larry Walsh. And so she had. Mae had said it might be a good way to resolve all those pent up feelings Martha had about the past. A woman had answered the phone and Martha almost hung up, but instead she asked for Larry. Hearing his voice brought back many more memories and almost made her want to cry — those pent up feelings, she figured.

She rinsed out the cloth and folded it neatly by the sink then headed upstairs to find a dress. He was scheduled to arrive at seven giving her just under an hour to get ready. Martha rummaged through her closet pulling out one dress after another and, with every one, found an excuse why she couldn't wear it: too small, too bright, too flowery, too low-cut, too short. She didn't want to think of how many pounds she had gained since he had last seen her. Finally, she settled on a pale pink blouse and a straight black skirt. Not too bright, not too staid. When the curling iron was hot, she sat at her dressing table and tightened her short curls, frizzy from the day's heat. In the mirror, she could see her hands shaking. She laid down the hot iron and comb, clutched her hands together, closed her eyes and prayed.

"Lord, help me." She asked again for forgiveness for treating

Larry so badly all those years ago and for the strength to face him this evening. As she sat with her eyes closed, Martha felt heat creeping across her chest and up to her face. "Oh no!" she shrieked. Quickly, she stood up and took off her blouse so it wouldn't get drenched in sweat. She stood in her bra and skirt fanning her body with a magazine and cursing the timing of her hormonal surge. At five minutes before seven, her hair wasn't finished, and there was no telling how long before her body cooled down. Now she prayed Larry would be late. She went back to work on her hair, unhappy with the outcome when finished. Just as she tucked her blouse back into her skirt, the door chimes rang. Martha descended the stairs and stood listening to the chimes ring once again then, with a deep breath, she opened the door.

Larry had changed dramatically. Thinner, his hair darker and longer and his cheeks not so full, but Lord have mercy, those blue eyes were as charming as she remembered. Instantly, her hand covered her open mouth and tears filled her eyes. He held a bouquet of pink carnations and yellow roses. She began to laugh at how foolish she surely appeared.

"Oh, goodness, please come in. You didn't have to get me flowers."

His smile broadened, that familiar dimple creasing his left cheek; he remained standing at the door. He closed his eyes for a moment then inhaled deeply before stepping inside and offering her the bouquet.

"You're as lovely as you always were, Martha."

Unable to speak, she took the flowers, buried her face in their fragrance and shook her head not believing his words or that he was truly at her door. She led him into the sitting room and offered him a drink — she wasn't a drinker herself but had a bottle of brandy that someone had given her years ago. He accepted and as she poured the drink, she almost poured one for herself. Instead, she got a ginger ale, found a vase and placed the flowers on the coffee table. He sat in the middle of her couch holding his drink and she took a seat in the armchair opposite. He wore a light-blue cotton shirt and black pants; they looked new, or fresh out of the

Laundromat. They sat smiling at each other, not believing they were together again.

"I'm real glad you called me," Larry said. "Real glad." She expected him to say more, but he fell silent and simply gazed at her. She patted her hair and looked at her feet. She still wore her blue furry slippers. Her cheeks flushed and again she laughed at herself.

"I forgot to put on my shoes," she said.

He chuckled at her footwear. "I bet they're way more comfortable than your shoes, anyhow."

Again, they both laughed and sipped their drinks. Martha was still shaking but knew someone would have to start the conversation about their past. "Larry, I, uh … I'm sorry that I shut you out of my life. Not letting you be a father to Kira. I am truly sorry for that."

He nodded. "Well, I wasn't exactly pounding at your door to see her. But I shoulda been." He shrugged. "What's done is done."

"Kira said you met each other, but it didn't go so well."

"It was a shock for her," he said, watching Martha closely. "She thought I was dead, and didn't know I was white."

Martha heaved a sigh. He wasn't accusing her, but she knew he wanted an explanation.

"I was young and foolish, Larry. I don't know what else to say." She had cherished the time they had spent together, and told him so, but it was harder to explain why she had wanted him to disappear. "With a child it just seemed … harder with you being, you know, white and all." Martha swirled the ice around in her glass. "I don't think I was ready to fight that battle."

Again, he nodded. "I didn't mean to stir things up by coming back. You've been on my mind, both of you. Seems as I get older, I'm thinking more and more about the past."

Martha couldn't agree more. These days memories were quick to surface. She remembered Larry serenading her on his trumpet as they sat in his car, watching the stars and the city lights from the Blue Ridge Parkway.

"Do you still play the trumpet?"

"Nah. My life ain't been that easy. I brought most of my troubles on myself."

After he received an honorable discharge from the Army, he moved to Tennessee where a cousin got him a job working on cars in an auto repair shop. It wasn't long before he got bored with the monotony of the repairs and headed out to California where he married a hairdresser. He had tried to settle down into marriage, but the routine bored him. He joined a jazz band to recapture his youth, but after only sixteen months the group struggled to make ends meet and fell apart. By then he had left his wife and was living with a young actress. He began experimenting with drugs, and in the Los Angeles nightlife, he lost himself to the allure of cocaine.

"Time just disappeared on me," he said. "It was like being in prison, 'cept nobody put you there but yourself. Some friends helped me get into a rehab clinic and I finally got my act together. It was shame that kept me from coming back to Virginia. Folks thought I'd be somebody. And look at me now."

His frankness surprised Martha, yet further endeared him to her.

"We all dream that we're going to be famous and rich," she said. "And then life takes hold and before you know it thirty years have passed you by."

He took a short sip of his brandy and continued telling his story, as if compelled to report back to Martha all the details of his life since leaving her. After his grandparents passed away, his parents moved from Fort Lewis to the family home in Nashville. Larry moved back from California to Knoxville to be closer to them without being too close. That was when he got his license to drive eighteen-wheelers and started his own business hauling products up and down the East Coast. He liked being on the road — gave him a sense of freedom he hadn't experienced anywhere other than when he was playing music.

"I look back and wonder what I contributed to the world, and it seems like nothing at all," he said.

"We all contribute something to the world. We just don't always find out what it is."

They began to reminisce about their short time together, about the nightclub and about whatever happened to the other band members Larry had played with. Before long, they were both laughing and recounting one story after another. Martha reminded Larry of the first night he had come to chat with her. He was so busy trying to impress by recounting his meeting with Fats Domino that he didn't hear Mike, the band's lead singer, call for Larry to get back on stage. Everyone in the club was whooping and hollering at Larry until he finally realized they were all calling out to him. While he had the audience's attention, Larry gently placed the trumpet to his lips and serenaded Martha, whose cheeks turned the color of black cherries. Sitting in her home, she felt the heat rise in her face at the memory and giggled all the harder.

Martha didn't hear Kira enter through the back door. Not until she was standing in the doorway between the kitchen and the sitting room did Martha see her. Larry instinctively stood up as if he and Martha had been caught doing something illicit. Kira stared at them both, all three saying nothing. Kira started to speak then stopped, swiveled suddenly and disappeared into the dark kitchen and out the back door. Martha wasn't quick enough to catch her daughter, whose vehicle was already speeding down the street. When she returned to the sitting room, Larry was still standing and wringing his hands.

"I should go," he said.

"Oh, don't feel like you have to go," she said, returning to her seat. "You talked about making mistakes in your life. Well, I guess we've both been foolish in our own ways."

They sat only a moment longer before Larry insisted he should go. Martha was sad to see him leave, and frustrated that her daughter was being so quick to dismiss him. His life had moved along a path far different from hers, yet they had connected once again as they had done all those years ago, finding pleasure in each other's company. She couldn't help but imagine what their lives would have been like had she allowed him back into her life to actively be Kira's father. While it was fun to consider the possibility of happiness with him for all these years, she knew too well, Larry never would have been content to stay in one place for long. Still, she was glad they had finally tried to fill the gap.

Before heading to bed, Martha said a prayer that her daughter would eventually find some solace in her father's reappearance.

26

A LEX HAD spent the past two weeks working on it and now was proud to be finished, just in time for his father's birthday. He lifted the piece up with both hands and angled it in the light. He had transformed the block of wood into a plate to hang on the wall, about two feet in diameter with the faces of his grandfather, father, himself and Andy carved into it, each face blending into the other. Three generations of Harper men. Meticulously, he had brought the chunk of black walnut alive with his own image and those of the three men he most revered. As the elder, PawPaw was in the center. Alex gently placed it on his working table and caressed the faces, confident Paw would love it. MawMaw had invited a few of his father's friends over for cake after dinner to celebrate, and he would present it to him then.

Alex closed the shop, letting his father leave early. He wrapped the gift in brown paper and carefully carried it to the truck, placing it on the passenger seat, where he left it while he ate dinner with his family. His uncle Matt had driven in from Nashville, where he had his own construction company. Matt wasn't an uncle by blood, but had been such a close childhood friend of Richard's that Alex had grown up calling him Uncle Matt. As dinner ended and more visitors stopped in, mostly to get a piece of MawMaw's delicious dessert, they joked, than to wish Richard a happy birthday. Alex slipped outside to retrieve the gift — too big to hide behind his back — and as he entered the sitting room, PawPaw drew everyone's attention to it by asking Alex what he had in his arms. Alex felt a sudden rush of anxiety that surprised him.

"Well, PawPaw, it's something I've put a lot of hours and love into for this man right here," he said, grinning at his father who stood with an empty paper plate, streaked with icing he hadn't licked clean. Richard frowned. Alex knew his father wasn't big on being the center of attention unless heading a committee or introducing someone else. Alex held out the heavy parcel. Elaine grabbed Richard's plate, freeing his hands to accept the offering. His father hesitated then took the gift and unwrapped it, letting the paper float to the floor. He stared at the gift. Alex detected a slight furrow in his father's brow. His breathing became shallow and all but his father disappeared around him. The silence was infuriating. Rising disappointment filled his chest. Now he understood his anxiety. Though he hadn't expected his father to scream with delight, the man's empty expression was unbearable. This was the most powerful piece he had created since coming home and he wanted only his father to have it. The room began to move again when MawMaw came close and exclaimed how beautiful the piece was, how Alex had captured his grandfather so perfectly.

"Isn't it uncanny how they all look so alike," she said to the room. Exclaiming oohs and ahhs, people gathered around Richard to see Alex's creation, but still, Richard said nothing. Finally, he handed the plate to Uncle Matt who was expressing his amazement at Alex's ability to capture everyone's likeness in wood. Richard wandered away toward the back of the house. Alex turned to leave and almost walked into his grandfather. Big Bear placed his large callused hand on his grandson's shoulder.

"It ain't about you, Alex," he said. "He's thinking back is all. He's got two sons on that plate and only one able to stand with him in this room. You know your father, he won't say nothing to nobody about what he's feeling. But don't think he don't appreciate it. He does."

Alex tried to feel better, tried to understand his father's pain and know that he did love the gift. He walked out onto the front porch, making sure the screen door didn't crash against the frame, and sat on the old swing.

Fifteen years had passed since Andy had died. A death in the family is tough to recover from, but when would his father realize he needed to show fatherly love to his living son? He felt a nudge in his gut to leave everything behind. Maybe he should leave for good this time? He left the swing and walked out into the darkness. Bats darted across the navy blue sky and small animals scampered through the bushes. He kept walking until he came to Winston's home. A warm glow radiated from the two-story wooden frame house; lights glowed from almost every window. Alex hesitated before knocking on the door.

Tessa welcomed him inside with a hug and a kiss. Alex gently patted her belly and joked that she had gotten a beach ball stuck under her shirt. She laughed; only two more months till the due date, she said. Winston sat in his chair, the one closest to the television, focused on a baseball game, his worried expression indicating a moment of tension in the play. Winston held a beer bottle in his right fist and gestured for Alex to take a seat on the couch while keeping his eyes on the screen. The pitcher wound his arm and threw a fastball. The batter blew the ball into the left-center field bleachers. Winston moaned at the screen then looked forlornly at Alex.

"That's his second homer against my guys," he said. "What's up with you? Aren't you supposed to be celebrating you pops' birthday?"

"It's all his old friends. Figured I'd get out of there for awhile."

"Did he like the gift?"

Alex had kept the gift a secret from everyone except Winston. He respected his friend's artistic eye and over the years they had often sought each other's opinion on a new piece they had created. "Yeah, he liked it."

The pair watched the game as Winston's children, despite the late hour, provided background noise as they fought and played on the floor. Tessa brought Alex a cold beer and slapped Winston across the back of his head for not doing it himself. Winston shot back that Alex knew where to find the fridge. Tessa shook her head then disappeared back into the kitchen where Alex could hear her chatting on the telephone. When the game finally ended Winston announced he had something for Alex to see. They descended to the basement, which Winston had transformed into a studio.

"I stole your idea," Winston said.

An easel displayed a watercolor of Tessa with their two boys and daughter: the children's faces surrounding their mother.

"It's not as good as the carving. I gotta work on it some more, but it looks pretty cool, don't you think?"

"You got a beautiful family," Alex said.

"Maybe I should wait till the baby is born."

Alex suggested he have Tessa cradling the baby with the three kids behind her. Winston nodded his agreement.

"So what did your pops say when you gave him the plate?"

Alex stared at the painting of Winston's family trying to envision himself with a wife and children. Then he looked at his friend and told him his father had said nothing at all.

"PawPaw said it made him sad to see Andy's face again."

"That's understandable. Although he coulda said something to show he liked the gift."

Alex shrugged.

"Tessa said she heard you and Lorett broke up."

Typical that Lorett would tell people he had ended the relationship. She liked being dramatic that way.

"I don't know if it's over. I told her I needed a break. Time to think. Winston, I'm just not sure about this whole marriage thing. You and Tessa are happy, but I think about Dave and how miserable he is and what happened to my folks—"

"That don't mean the same thing's gonna happen to you. If you're not sure, it's best to seriously think about it. The worst is getting into it when you're not certain. Me, I was sure the first time I set eyes on Tess. She was beautiful, man." He chuckled. "There was no way I was gonna let any other man snap her up."

"You're lucky."

"Nah, not luck. Hard work."

Alex asked if Tessa had seen the painting. She hadn't. Winston decided he would add the fourth child and present it to her as a gift after the baby was born. They sat for a while longer chatting about

their work and baseball until Tessa yelled down that she was heading to bed.

"She hates going to bed by herself," Winston said. "I could sit
up all night sometimes, but more than ever these days, she gets real
grouchy when things don't go her way." He paused on the way up
the stairs and in a hushed voice said, "See, when I say it's work, this
is what I mean. You gotta know your battles."

A FULL moon filled the night with shadows that followed Alex
home. A cool breeze wrapped itself around him as he walked; the
dusty dirt road muffled each step while his thoughts drifted.
Interesting that Lorett was saying they were no more. He knew she
would make him out to be the bad guy, and maybe he was the bad
guy. He had been surprised when she hadn't been in touch. Usually
after a fight she waited only a day or two before she called asking
to make up. Usually, he said okay. This time, he assumed her
silence meant she was truly giving him space, but now he knew she
was using the grapevine to make him feel guilty. If she were trying
to trick him into begging for a reconciliation, she would be sorely
disappointed.

Maybe he would call Kira and explore his interest in her. He
had resisted getting back in touch, afraid of repeating the same
mistake he had made too many times before: finding a lover just
for fun, and falling in love only to discover some hidden reason
they couldn't be together. He would have easily spent the rest of his
life with Gloria, but he knew about her marriage when they met.
Maybe that had been part of the appeal — that he couldn't get
trapped.

27

KIRA BEGAN her short drive home but instead of turning off the main road, she kept going toward Vauseville. All the way, she tried to convince herself she simply wanted to follow up with the fundraising efforts, perhaps write another story. She practiced what to say, and silently hoped Alex would be there.

SHE ARRIVED just as Richard Harper was turning the "Closed" sign. He welcomed her warmly and she apologized for arriving at the end of the afternoon without calling. He told her the Floyd Nature Preserve had shown interest in the story and that he and the committee were in negotiations regarding a possible matching grant. The agreement would include keeping a large portion of the land as a natural wildlife habitat, which, Richard said, would hardly be a concession.

Alex came down the stairs and appeared through the curtain asking his father a question that stopped mid-sentence when he saw Kira.

THEY SAT on a boulder at the river's edge with a view of the valley, her fear that he would reject her washed away with the stream. She rested her head on his shoulder and he cradled her back with his arm. The mountains beyond were ablaze as the orange ball of sun melted like sherbet behind them. With eyes closed, she listened to the first few crickets to come alive. This moment, this peace and calm that surrounded him, she wanted to capture forever.

"This will sound like a stupid question, but what's it like being a Native American around here?" she asked.

"It's not stupid. I don't know any more about being black around here than you would about being Indian." He shrugged. "It's not so bad here in Vauseville. There are more of us here. I guess you would say we're kinda segregated." He reached his hand to her face and touched her cheek with the tips of his fingers so gently it felt like a feather. "What's it like being two races?"

Her heart stopped for a second. Two races. Hearing someone acknowledge aloud that she was mixed sounded odd, as if it had been a secret no one else should know. "Weird," she said. "I used to wonder what part of Africa my ancestors came from, what tribe they belonged to. Because my skin is so light I used to imagine I was from Egyptian royalty. I couldn't have been any farther from the truth."

She struggled to describe exactly what she felt — certainly disconnected from her childhood fantasies. In reality, though, nothing had changed. Her childhood memories remained the same — she had grown up in the black neighborhood on Richmond Avenue, had gone to school at North High, had studied at Virginia State, and now worked as a news reporter in her hometown. She was not a different person, yet the knowledge had placed her in no man's land. Would her past have changed if she had known her father? What made people who they were, anyway — genetics or environment? Was it the ability to firmly identify with a particular group or race, to have a culture and history to hold on to, or something else?

"I guess the difference between you and me is that you not only know who your ancestors are, but you know what was taken from your people."

"Maybe that's to your advantage. Your people can draw strength from what they've created for themselves in a land that's foreign to their ancestors."

"But now, I have to choose which culture to draw strength from."

"Do you have to choose?" he said, rising and pulling Kira up with him. "C'mon."

They headed to an old farmhouse that had been converted into a restaurant. Down Home served genuine home cooking, according to the sign. Now that the peak dinner hours were over the place wasn't busy. When they entered, they received glances from the few customers still there. Kira silently noted the only other black person in the place was a teenager clearing tables. An elderly couple sat near the back, dressed like a stereotypical older couple from the country, denim overalls on the man and a floral print dress on the woman, but a tint to the skin and a sharpness to the nose suggested to Kira they were Native Americans.

Alex found a window booth and they slid into the seats opposite each other. Tiny candles were lit on each table with dried flowers around the bases. Quaint. The menu listed basic meat and potatoes fare, so Kira chose the chicken pot pie and Alex selected the roast beef and mashed potatoes. A long time passed and no one came to take their order. A dark-headed boy stared at Kira while he swung his legs, bumping the heels against his chair. He sat at a table in the middle of the restaurant with his parents and a younger sibling. Kira gave him what she thought was a pleasant smile, but the boy continued his even stare. Alex nodded to a blonde waitress who acknowledged him with a lift of her chin before disappearing into the kitchen. She reappeared with a notepad.

"Yes?"

Kira thought the woman's attitude was stiff and reluctant but said nothing and placed her order. When the blonde left them, Kira leaned forward and whispered to Alex, "Is it you, or me?"

"Both probably. We should've gone into the city. Folks around here are funny about mixed couples. Some Indians don't like us mixing with black. Some older ones still resent being classified as black. Back then it meant inferior."

"So mixing with white is better?"

"Absolutely. Of course, sticking with your own is preferred.

Especially with some of the whites around here, although it depends. Sometimes being Indian is in, sometimes it's out."

The elderly man wandered over to the table. "Hey there Alex. How are ya? How's your pa?"

"I'm fine Mr. Hicks. Paw's doing all right."

The conversation lulled but the man remained standing at the table's edge making furtive glances at Kira. Alex caught the hint. "This is Kira Franklin," he said. "She's the reporter who did the story on us."

Finally, the man looked directly at her with a small smile. "Fine story that was." He turned back to Alex. "She writing another piece?"

"Possibly an update."

The man continued to engage Alex in conversation, asking about where things stood with the land, how much had been raised so far. He asked about Lorett and Alex assured him she was fine. After a long stretch of silence, he left, telling Alex to send his regards to his family. As the old man padded away toward the restrooms, Alex revealed that Mr. Hicks was the community gossip.

The waitress brought their meals, which lived up to the outdoor sign's pronouncement. They ate quietly and, despite Kira's protests, Alex left a tip. He apologized as if he were responsible for the luke-warm service.

"It's okay. We could've done worse in Fort Lewis. There are some black folks I wouldn't want to see us holding hands." She reached up to kiss his cheek, and before she could plant her lips, he gripped her waist and kissed her mouth. Reluctantly, she pulled away and as she did so a middle-aged white woman scurried past them muttering something about folks having no sense of shame. Alex and Kira looked back at each other and burst out laughing.

They decided to head back to Kira's place, and Alex followed her in his father's truck.

On her living room floor, his mouth closed over hers as he lifted her hips off the floor, pushing into her and sending lightning through her soul. They lay for a long time, stuck to each other as they stared at the white ceiling until sleep snuggled close. Kira felt his chest rise and fall. She didn't want this man to leave her. She wanted him to stay and hold her all night long like he had done before. For so long, she had been content to have men drift in and out of her life, but this man warmed her like a freshly laundered bathrobe, comfortable and delicious, and she wanted to preserve the sensation. Yet wanting someone to stay scared her.

Alex inhaled deeply and opened his eyes, looked at her, dazed for a moment as if unsure of his whereabouts, then a slight smile brightened his eyes and his lips pressed against her forehead. He wanted water and peeled away from her. Kira watched him walk to the kitchen and delighted in the way his hair swayed with his naked body. His back was damp and some strands were glued to his skin. He raked his fingers through his hair as he gulped a tall glass of water, refilled the glass and returned to Kira. She sat with her arms hugging her knees. He stretched out on the floor, leaning back on his left elbow and handed her the glass. After a short sip, she carefully placed the glass on the floor then giggled, suddenly nervous in the dim light of her sitting room. The bulb over the stove gave the room a warm glow and the table lamp in the corner seemed to shine in her face like a spotlight. She wanted to turn it off, to get it out of her eyes. It made her feel exposed.

Alex grabbed her ankles with a quickness that startled her and pulled her to him. He sat cross-legged and wrapped her legs around his waist then rested his head on her shoulder. "Thank you," he whispered.

"For what?"

"For being here for me."

He ran his fingers up and down her spine and Kira shivered. He lifted his head and peered at her face. "Are you nervous?"

"No," she said defensively. "A little cold, maybe."

Alex laughed deeply, making her smile. "Cold? It's ninety degrees outside and it doesn't feel like you have air conditioning. You're nervous." He began massaging the back of her neck.

She explained that the A/C unit broke earlier in the week and that someone was scheduled to fix it, and insisted that she was not nervous. He insisted that she was.

"It's kinda late to lose your nerve, isn't it?"

She looked at him, trying to appear blasé. "Lose my nerve about sleeping with you? Hardly. I just feel—" Afraid was the word that came to her lips but she stopped before releasing it into the air. Alex pulled back from her.

"You want me to leave?"

"No. Of course not. This feels good." She squeezed her thighs enjoying his skin against hers. After a while, his silence compelled her to speak, to try to explain herself. "This is different for me," she said. "I'm used to groping around in the dark then falling asleep and waking up alone."

"We're all at our most vulnerable when we make love." He let his fingers twirl her hair at the back of her head. "In the dark, sex is just a physical act between any two people. But with light, we can share more."

"And why do you want to share more with me? This probably isn't a good time to bring it up, but you are engaged to someone else."

Alex looked away from her. Kira shifted her weight but his arms tightened around her; his head returned to her shoulder. She tried to pull away but his grip constricted her movement. She didn't want him to belong to someone else. It wasn't fair.

"Let me go," she said.

He squeezed one last time then loosened his grip and she pushed herself upright with both hands. "Are you staying? Because if not, I gotta get some sleep." The words tumbled out of her, cutting him as they fell. He looked at her as if she had slapped him across his face, but she kept silent, fighting the urge to say sorry and go back to the warmth of his body. He stared at her until she couldn't stand it anymore, and she disappeared into the bathroom. When she returned moments later wearing a robe, he was dressed and searching for his boots. Kira wouldn't beg him to stay, although she wanted him to. She felt desperate to make him stay, but she wouldn't. She had never begged a man for anything in her life. If he wanted to leave, she wouldn't stop him. He didn't look at her. Not once as he slipped on his boots or when he tied his hair back behind his head. He lingered in the room looking at the floor for something else to appear that perhaps he had forgotten, then he turned and paused once more at the door before turning the knob.

"I didn't mean to say that," Kira blurted. She didn't want to beg.

A long time passed while he stood at the door not moving until slowly, gracefully, he opened the door and slipped out. She wanted to cry, yet didn't want to, wanted to run after him, but knew she wouldn't. Her guard had been down. Better that he leave her now before he had the chance to smash her heart later.

～

SEVERAL DAYS passed and Kira kept a low profile, staying focused on her work and spending her evenings at home. Late one afternoon, Beverly peered over the low partition of Kira's cubicle. She had news about Peter. After negotiating a lucrative severance package, in return for not suing the newspaper, he was establishing his own photography business and pursuing work with a corporate client. Kira was pleased; Pete deserved a great new start. Beverly continued to hover. Finally, she said: "Mom's taking Tamika to a kid's play at the church tonight. You want to grab a drink?"

They found an open spot at the bar of a local restaurant and ordered cocktails. They talked about their co-workers, complained about management, and discussed the latest news: Isn't it amazing that South Africa is only now agreed to multi-racial elections? Incredible! Did you see Canada has its first woman prime minister? That'll never happen in America, not in our lifetimes at least. What about that woman, Lorena Bobbitt, in Manassas who cut off her husband's penis? Bet he deserved it! They both laughed. An awkward silence crept between them as they surveyed the busy restaurant. Kira ordered another round of drinks.

"So, did you ever decide on what to do about Jamal?" asked Beverly.

Jamal had left messages for Kira, whining about her sudden disinterest in him after all the money he had spent on her. His first voice message had made her sad and regret her decision to leave him, but his second call later the same day only made her regret she had stayed with him for two years. The bastard had called her a selfish bitch. All she said to Beverly was: "It's over."

Beverly expressed her dismay but Kira shrugged it off.

"I hate men," Kira said.

"Really?"

Not really. What Kira hated was the confusing and complex nature of relationships with men. "Why is it so hard for us to be with someone?" she said, although she wasn't thinking about Jamal. She thought about Alex.

Beverly stared at her for several moments. "Okay, I'm going to tell you something." She took a long sip of her drink. "I've been seeing Pete for the last couple weeks."

Kira was speechless. In a rush, Beverly gushed about their first date several days after his firing. She had called to check in on him, make sure he was okay and had invited him out for a drink to cheer him up. "I've always liked him, but I didn't think he'd see me as anything more than a friend, but we've been out on several dates already, to the movies, to dinner, and even a night out dancing."

While Kira was truly thrilled that her friend was finally involved with a decent man who would likely cherish and respect her, she felt sad that their friendship had slipped so far apart that they both had been harboring secrets from each other instead of immediately sharing them.

She asked: "Why didn't you tell me?" Although she knew neither one had made an effort to resolve the hurt created from Beverly's relationship with Tony.

"Well, I just…"

"No, it's okay. I understand. I've been keeping my own secrets. I've wanted to tell you, but the moment never seemed right." So she talked frankly about the chaos in her life, starting with her father and ending with Alex. Somewhere in the midst of her words, she began to cry, overcome by her own outpouring and apologized for being foolish. Beverly held her hand and hushed Kira as she would her upset child.

"These two men have come into my life, complete opposites from one another," Kira said. "They're both culturally different from me and I don't know how to relate to either one of them. I don't know what I'm supposed to do, how to act, how to be, and yet I'm connected to them. But I'm afraid to let either one of them get to know me, to *really* get to know me."

"Why? What's your fear?

"What if I don't meet their expectations?"

Beverly contemplated her response. "Maybe they don't have any. Maybe you're the one with all the expectations and you're afraid they won't meet yours?"

Her friend's words stung, but perhaps Beverly was right. Kira thought about the image she had created in her mind of her father. Had *that* sophisticated African American walked into her life, would she have been so hasty to reject him? And what if Alex were available? Could she seriously consider a future with a man from a different race and culture?

She thanked Beverly for listening and congratulated her on discovering a romance with a man who had been practically under her nose for the past three years.

For the rest of the evening, Kira pondered what to do about these two men she seemed determined to push away.

28

A LEX BANGED his fist on Dave's trailer door and the entire unit shook. He stood on a makeshift stoop — a wooden platform held up by cinderblocks. High weeds crept out from under the mobile home, inching their way up to the windows and wrapping around the rear end of a bicycle, apparently abandoned beneath the trailer years ago. Dogs barked somewhere nearby. The trailer was one of a long line of white mobile homes in a trailer park just south of Vauseville. Three rows of white rectangles covered several acres, distinctive only by the entrances, which varied from elaborate patios to simple brick steps. Bill Petitt, a banker who lived in a large brick house in Fort Lewis, owned the lot and sold the units in co-op fashion. Dave shared the trailer with his brother.

Alex banged again. A silver-haired lady came out of the unit across the dirt road and emptied a pan of greasy water over the banister of her wooden deck. He called over to her. "You seen Dave?"

"Not since yesterday." Wiping her free hand on her skirt, she said, "Ain't been no comings or goings that I've noticed."

"Not even Thomas?"

"Nuh uh." The woman shook the pan one last time before disappearing indoors.

Alex stood staring at the door as if any minute it would open. Dave's truck was parked in its space, but his brother's Mustang was gone. Alex decided to knock one more time then head to Lakeside by himself. Winston would likely be there already. Impulsively, Alex gripped the door handle and yanked on it. The door jerked open. He stood baffled, thinking it shouldn't have been so easy to get in. He called Dave's name and stepped inside. The buzz of flies came from the kitchenette, where glasses and plates were piled up around the sink. Gunfire rattled out of a movie on the television and Dave lay comatose on the couch, one foot resting on the floor, the other propped up on the armrest.

"Jesus, Dave." Alex pulled the footstool close to the couch and sat down. The stench of liquor was overpowering. Fortunately, the man's snore confirmed that Dave was still in the land of the living, although barely so. An empty bottle of Jack Daniels lay on the floor, the top nowhere in sight. Alex slapped his friend's face on each cheek and waited for a response. In the bathroom, he found a green washcloth hanging on the shower rod and rinsed it in cold water. He returned to Dave's side and smacked him with the cold cloth. This time Dave spluttered awake.

"Goddamn! What the hell you doing?" He swatted the air as if mosquitoes were attacking him.

Alex chuckled, relieved to see his friend come awake. "How long have you been passed out like this, man?"

"Thomas?"

Alex smacked Dave's face one more time and instinctively Dave's fist flew out, missing Alex by more than a foot. Shaking his head, Alex repeated his question. Dave sat up, rested his elbows on his knees and held his head in his hands. "Alex, brother, I'm sorry. I thought you were Thomas. I been on the couch a couple hours, I guess."

"A couple hours?" Alex was skeptical. "You go to work today?"

"Huh?"

"Work, man. At the construction site."

Dave wiped his palms across his face and shook his head.

"You're gonna lose another one if you're not careful. Where's Thomas?"

"He's probably at Maggie's place. He spends most of his time there these days."

"I'm thinking we don't need to go to Lakeside tonight. How about I get some coffee and bring you back something to eat?"

"Nah, let's go to Lakeside. I need to get out and have me some fun."

Alex shook his head. He searched the room for the phone and, finding it under the coffee table, called the club, asking for Winston. He explained Dave's condition and Winston offered to bring some chicken dinners and coffee.

"What's the matter with you, man?" Alex asked, returning to the stool.

Dave said nothing.

"This isn't the Dave I knew. Don't tell me this is still about losing Phoebe? You gotta get over that."

"That's easy for you to say," Dave snapped back, rubbing his temples. "You got a woman who'll wait for you for years while you're off sowing your oats. It don't matter what you do, she's always gonna be there, no matter how you treat her. You take her for granted like she's nothing, but she'll take you back. Why? Cause your family's got power."

"Power? Are you kidding me?"

"It might not be like state governor, but in this shit-hole town, it means something. Me, I got nothing. I ain't ever gonna be somebody, and women don't want a loser like me."

Dave again covered his face with his hands and continued to mumble into them about not having his own place, having to come home to his baby brother's trailer, that Thomas owned his own car and was engaged to a good-looking woman. Alex kept silent, letting his friend vent. He watched the man he had known since childhood when they had swapped comic books and shared gumballs. Nothing he could say would make Dave feel better. Alex had never expected either of them to become wealthy businessmen but figured they would each have a respectable life. He hadn't expected Dave to become a drunk. After high school, Dave had simply wanted to get a decent-paying job and live happily-ever-after with Phoebe. He used the phrase often, especially at the end of a conversation about their futures, "My story ends happily-ever-after with Phoebe," he'd say. They had been together throughout most of high school, as Alex and Lorett had been. Winston, on the other hand, had dated one girl after another, placing little thought on his future, including marriage. How ironic, Alex thought, that Winston would be the one to settle down and have a large family.

"I've got nothing. Nothing to offer no one and no prospects in sight," Dave mumbled.

Alex patted his friend's shoulder. It didn't seem fair that this should be Dave's existence, yet surely he could change it if he put his mind to it? The thought of ending up a drunk living alone didn't appeal to Alex. Ending up alone had never occurred to Alex; he had assumed someone would be there for him, because someone *had* always been there. Miscellaneous lovers, and when they were gone, Dave was right: there had always been Lorett. No matter what, she had never wavered in her patience. But was that enough reason to marry her? What was the existence of men without women? Was he looking at it now, this discarded soul continuing to pine for his love and drowning in alcohol? Surely Dave didn't have to live this way.

"It's your choice, Dave," Alex said. "You can decide to spend your paycheck on beer and bourbon or start saving for a home and a decent car. Call yourself a loser if you want to, but you're the only one who can change that."

Dave continued to sulk, while Alex thought about his advice and wondered if these were words he should be telling himself.

∽

THE PIGEON stretched its neck backwards sticking its beak into its ruffled feathers. It preened and fussed over itself then settled as if to take a nap. Another bird fluttered onto the roof almost toppling the first as it swooped in so close. It turned and settled itself as if to nap with its friend. Kira sipped her coffee and watched the birds on the neighboring roof from the diner's window. How sweet they looked. How so in love. Kira closed her eyes.

With two hours before her interview with the church pastor,

she had headed out to the diner because it always offered an array of fascinating characters to watch. Today, though, she felt restless and rummaged through her purse for Larry Walsh's phone number. She wasn't too far from Brighton Place where he said he was staying. Should she make amends? If her mother could accept him, why not she? The phone in the parking lot was out of order so she drove the few miles to Brighton Place hoping his truck would show the way. She saw no sign of a big rig parked on the quiet street. Kira stared at the old brick houses surrounded by uncut hedges and rusted wire fences. Broken furniture and corroded cars decorated dusty yards, but nothing gave away a sign of where she could find Larry Walsh. She wondered if she had misheard him, then noticed a wrinkled black man sitting on his front stoop. It was worth a try to ask him. The old man didn't know Larry Walsh, but an eighteen-wheeler had been parked at the other end of the street for a week or so.

"It ain't none o' my business, mind," he said, "but it might be that I seen a white man entering Clara McDaniel's house on the corner."

As she walked up the path, Kira saw someone pull at the curtain and the door had opened by the time she reached it. A shiny, dark-skinned woman with curlers in her hair stood half hidden behind the door. Smoking a cigarette, she blew the smoke outside and squinted through the crack.

"I'm Kira." She was intrigued that Larry Walsh was staying with a black woman and wondered if that was his preference in women.

"I figured as much," the woman said.

"Is Larry here? I know it's early. I'm sorry. I was nearby and thought I'd say hey."

"He ain't here. He's gone." The woman blew another puff of smoke out the door.

"Sorry for disturbing you." Kira took a step back. "When he gets back, can you tell him I came by?"

"Nah, girl, I mean he's gone. It could be months before I see him again."

Kira stared at the woman.

"Old Larry ain't gonna stay nowhere for no time. Besides he gotta get back to the clinic before too long."

"The clinic?"

The woman blinked slowly and looked at the weeds pushing their way through the cracks in the concrete. She picked something out of her teeth with her long fingernail and wiped it on her robe.

"He's sick?" Kira asked.

"He said he was gonna tell you." She backed away from the door. "Why don't you come in."

Kira hesitated, then entered the small house.

"Excuse the mess," the woman said, shuffling her way through crumpled magazines and papers on the floor into a kitchen. Dishes were piled in and around the sink and cigarette ash flowed from an ashtray on the table. "I'm Clara by the way. You want coffee?"

Kira shook her head and sat at a chair already pulled away from the table. Clara sat opposite her and tightened the belt on her gown.

"He got the AIDS. Been diagnosed for several months now. I figured he wouldn't tell you, but he said he would."

Numbness stretched across Kira's mind. She stared into the woman's deep black cheeks, then let her gaze drift around the room taking in empty beer bottles, an empty can of baked beans on the counter. Larry Walsh, the man who was her father, had AIDS. He could die before she saw him again. Dinner plates balanced on a stainless steel pot, grease covering the stove. He had wanted to see her before he died. A roach trap covered with dust balls lay in the corner of the floor. Maybe he was simply trying to make peace with the past. Pages from *The Fort Lewis Times* were scattered across the table. Clara's cigarettes and lighter reminded Kira of her meeting with him. She felt awful at having rejected him so quickly. Clara lit herself another cigarette but Kira didn't hear the offer to have one. She was wondering what he must think of her now, wondering if she could make amends. He had asked forgiveness, asked to make a fresh start. She han't seen the possibility then to start as friends.

"Please tell me where he is?" she asked, softly.

Clara inhaled deeply then blew smoke out the side of her mouth and attempted to fan it away from Kira. "I ain't for sure."

"Please."

The woman paused then rose with the enthusiasm of a turtle and disappeared into a back room. She returned with an address book overflowing with scraps of paper that had been added to its pages. Flopping back into her seat, she stared at Kira. "He'll know I gave this to you. Larry likes being invisible. Don't never want folks knowing where he is."

"So how come you know?"

"Everyone's gotta have an anchor somewhere." Clara scribbled on a corner of the newspaper and tore it off. "Here. He stays at this address most times with a man named Roscoe. That's where the clinic is, and I know he's gotta be back there soon for his check up." The address was an apartment in Knoxville, Tennessee. Kira nodded not knowing exactly what she would do with the information.

"I really appreciate this," she said, rising from the chair. "All my life I've wanted to know my father. And now, I might've messed up my only chance to get to know him."

"He talks about you sometimes. I think he's been scared of what you might think of him."

"I don't hate him." Kira's words were rushed as if she needed the woman to know, as if she needed to say it out loud so the world would know in case she never got the chance to tell him herself. Clara smiled and her round cheeks glistened. Kira returned her smile. "Thanks."

She sauntered to her Jeep. The old man was still on the stoop and she waved, quietly thanking him for his help. He would never know what he had done.

The door was open and she stepped inside. Peace settled over her as the door swung closed with a soft click. The dark wooden pews and beams gave the church a cozy feeling despite the high ceiling and tall stained glass windows. A massive wooden crucifix behind the altar held Kira's stare. Christ's eyes were dark brown and his skin creamy white. She thought about the actor with the bright blue eyes who had played Jesus Christ in a movie she had seen years ago. She looked at Christ's image on the wall and wondered if his skin had really been that pale. Their mother had seldom attended church when Kira and her brother were young, but in recent years Martha had devoted most of her time to the church. Although Kira's childhood memories of Easter Sunday and Christmas services were vague images of bows and new shoes, she rarely joined her mother for Sunday service. She rejected the notion that God existed. If there were an almighty God, why would He allow so much sadness in the world? God would have provided her and Kenny with a father who came home to them every night, who loved and cared for them every day. Surely their trials and their mother's tribulations were not part of God's plan? A plan that included enormous pain and hardship for so many people around the world? Was it God who had brought her father into her life just to take him away, who had created the likelihood that he would die from an incurable disease? What was the lesson in that?

Her father wasn't what she had expected, but she had to accept him. He had shared love with her mother, and that counted for something. Her anger had flared when seeing her mother comfortably laughing and talking with Larry Walsh as if they had been friends all those years. She had been angry at her mother for having lied about him for so long, angry that he wasn't the man she had dreamed, and angry at herself for feeling totally out of control. Now, Kira found herself deeply sorry for rejecting him and most likely throwing away any chance of knowing the man who had fathered her. Silently, she asked, "God, if you are there, can you make this right?"

The large door to the right of the altar clicked open, and Kira raised her head abruptly. The pastor walked slowly up the middle aisle toward her.

"I can give you more time if you need it," he said, smiling.

"I was just thinking."

"Thinking can turn into prayer, and prayer is good for the soul."

She nodded. "Perhaps, but I didn't come here to pray."

"You're Kira Franklin from the *Times*? It's a pleasure to meet you." His firm and comforting handshake made her feel at ease.

29

WIND WHIPPED through the cab of the truck as Alex sped along the highway back to Vauseville. He couldn't wait to see his father's face when he told him the news: a contract to sell his work in a store in the largest mall in Fort Lewis. Plus the chance to promote Big Bear's Cabin, and a new computer he had bought on credit in the spur of the moment. He couldn't wait to show off the computer and demonstrate the accounting program that would revolutionize the store and finally bring it into the modern world. Surely this would instill his father's confidence. He watched the sky along the horizon ahead of him. The clouds were like slow-moving cattle in varying shades of gray, moving across a bright blue plain. The morning's thunderstorm had gone to darker pastures and the sun made him smile. He parked outside the store and almost ran inside. He noted that his grandfather wasn't in his usual spot at the door, but dismissed it.

"Paw, I got some news."

Richard Harper was showing off a beaded necklace to a young woman and motioned to his son to wait a minute. A little girl of three or four trotted around the store shaking a leather anklet covered with bells, usually worn during ceremonial dances. Alex almost grabbed it from her, annoyed that he couldn't immediately surprise his father with the purchase. The woman, who was white, sought a birthday gift for her mother who was apparently part Indian. Alex shook his head at the woman's attempt to remember the tribe her great grandmother had come from. He took the bag with the software into the back room then propped the door open to bring the computer and the monitor inside. He managed to get the heavy boxes out of the truck, one at a time, without dropping them, through the store to the back and laid one gently on the chair and the other on the floor. The customer seemingly couldn't make up her mind between the beaded necklace and a silver arrowhead pendant inlaid with turquoise. The arrowhead was the better sale. Alex sauntered toward them.

"You say your great grandmother was Choctaw?" he said.

"Oh." The woman turned to face him. "You know that does sound familiar. That could've been it."

"Hmm." Alex affected a thoughtful expression. "You know, the Choctaw were known for their turquoise jewelry."

The woman's face brightened. "Is that right?"

"Uh-huh."

She studied the necklace more closely, running the chain through her fingers. "Well, I think I'll take this one then."

After the customer had corralled her daughter and left the store, gift in hand, Richard looked perplexed. "The Choctaw were known for their turquoise jewelry?"

Alex instantly launched into his story, his words tripping over themselves, about a friend of a friend who knew the manager of a craft shop in Fort Lewis who had expressed interest in seeing Alex's work for possible sale in the store. Alex not only secured the deal but took the opportunity to make sure Big Bear's Cabin was prominently featured in the shop. Richard nodded his approval but eyed the boxes as if they held two angry cougars ready to pounce.

"It's a computer," Alex said, ripping open the top of the box revealing the vented cream top of the monitor.

"I know what it is. I'm just wondering what it's doing in here?"

"Paw! We're gonna get with it. Get modern. This'll make our lives easier 'cause we'll—"

The phone rang just as Alex was about to school his father on the many ways the computer would enhance the business. Richard answered the call and remained silent for several moments, then he became agitated and his voice responded to the caller with single words. Alex heard the word "ambulance" and stepped closer. His father slammed the phone back in its cradle.

"It's your grandpaw. Lock up the store."

His father sped to the house, sharply cutting corners forcing Alex to grip his seat. They arrived shortly after the ambulance. Outside in his grandfather's vegetable garden, Alex watched the EMT pounding on the old man's chest. Alex recognized the young technician. Jesse lived over on Pine Ridge. Alex had gone to school with his older brother. Jesse finally stopped and sat motionless with his chin almost pressed against his chest. The air turned cold and his grandma's wail made every hair rise on Alex's face, his arms and his thighs. On her knees at her husband's side, she gripped his hand and rocked back and forth. One of the other technicians that Alex didn't know patted Richard's back. "I'm sorry, Mr. Harper."

Alex felt desperate to do something. "Why didn't you take him to the hospital?" He hadn't meant to shout but his voice didn't seem to be his own.

Jesse looked up. "I didn't get a pulse when we got here, but I tried anyway. I tried the best I could." He was on the verge of tears as he stood and approached Alex. "I'm sorry, man. I thought I could bring him back. I thought I could."

Alex held back the urge to scream. His PawPaw lay on his back, eyes open, staring blindly at the clouds drifting across the blue sky.

BY EARLY evening his grandparents' house was full of people. They had heard the news and came to offer their support and condolences. Dishes filled with food covered the kitchen as if it were Christmas. The chatter swarmed around his head suffocating him, so Alex stepped outside and started walking. He walked until he found himself standing outside the community center, its black windows staring down at him. So much of the place embodied his grandfather, from the idea to convert the old school building into a community center, to including an Indian museum. PawPaw had instigated the renovation and over the years had rallied a team of volunteers to maintain it. Alex took a seat on the front steps, rested his elbows on his knees and leaned forward. His hair fell like a curtain around his face shielding him from the world. He remembered getting caught by a group of white teenagers from a nearby town. They had been throwing rocks at cans balanced on a fence on the edge of the woods near PawPaw's house. Alex used to play in those woods. The teenagers spotted him and accused him of spying. He shook his head vigorously, backing away hoping they would leave him alone. But they took chase after him. Brandishing a pocketknife, one of the boys caught him by his hair when Alex slipped in the mud. They took turns trying to hack it off. "Your mama's a whore and your daddy's a drunk," hollered one. "Scalp him!" screamed another, followed by raucous laughter. Then Alex heard the distinctive sha-click of a shotgun. Everyone stopped. PawPaw stood only a few feet away and pointed the gun at the boys. "Get the hell off my property and don't come back, 'cause if you do, you ain't gonna survive next time."

His grandfather had come to his rescue more times than he could remember, most often saving him from his father's wrath. PawPaw had been his savior and his defender. Alex's teachers had complained to the principal that his hair was unruly, but rather than conform like many of his peers, he had kept it long, like his father and grandfather. His hair represented part of his heritage. Why couldn't he be like his brother, Andy, who had conformed, had fit in and was well liked by all? People refused to understand Alex, except PawPaw. PawPaw had always defended his right to be his own person.

"Never feel uncomfortable with who you are," he had said, "because who you are follows you to the grave."

Alex had been running all his life from uncertainties, from responsibilities, from the fire inside himself. Always crossing boundaries, shirking the inevitable. Yet now, it seemed all the more important to conform, to become the leader and husband his father expected. Only to do so was at odds with who he wanted to be. He didn't know how to be his own person *and* be the man his father wanted him to be. The tears splashed on the concrete steps, and Alex watched them make stars in the dust. He had never felt so alone.

HE HAD been driving around for several hours, through back roads, stopping on the high ridge to look at the lights of Fort Lewis and later joining the highway into the city. Alex found himself sitting outside Kira's home. The hour was near two o'clock in the morning, but there was no one else he wanted to be with. He knocked too quietly on her door for her to hear and wondered if he should simply leave. Would she let him inside? He had no idea how she felt about him. Again, he knocked harder and moments later she appeared, peeking through a crack in the door, covering a yawn and rubbing her eyes. She gaped at him a long time. He didn't know what to say. When she finally opened the door wide enough for him to get inside, he felt himself begin to crumble. He couldn't hold it together any longer. He fell to his knees and began to cry, covering his face with his fists, his body heaving with torrential sobs that rose from his gut. Her arms wrapped around his shoulders and he curled into her embrace, his grief continuing to release itself as he wept. As he grew calm he tried to explain, the words choking in his throat. She led him to the couch, brought him water and let him sit in silence. He didn't want to say the words aloud but knew that holding them in wouldn't change the truth.

"He's gone. PawPaw's gone." He reached for her again, burying his face in her stomach and clinging to her body, afraid to let go.

~

WARM RAIN fell, and Kira smelled the sour heat rise from the pavement. She sat in her Jeep watching people march across the grass to the gravesite. Children walked earnestly, clutching their elders with one hand and a token for the dead in the other. Suede and fringes swished their way to say goodbye in the rain. While some wore the traditional dark-colored funeral attire, Kira felt out of place in her navy blue pants suit. The colors of the mourners were mostly bright, earthy and elegant. She slid out of the vehicle and pushed open the black and white umbrella. Her heels sank into the sod as she walked across the wet grass. One hundred, maybe more gathered beneath and around the canopy covering the grave. Drummers sat a few feet away from the site, beating a slow rhythm that stirred her heart, and her eyes filled with tears. The rhythms and the lulled singing bid farewell to one whose passing would further distance the modern-day Virginia Cherokee from a past generation.

Kira felt awkward and intrusive, although she had received a call from Richard Harper inviting her to come. She felt compelled to be here. Strangely, the ceremony was comforting, even though it filled her with grief, not only for the man, but also for his ways and his people. This was the true picture of family: a community gathering to respect its elder. It gave her a sense of what it might feel like to be a part of something more sublime than the loneliness that comprised her life. Who would come to her funeral besides her mother, if she were still alive? Beverly? And would she be recognized for anything more than working at her hometown newspaper writing about the trivial and the absurd? There was history here among the Native Americans and a legacy of belonging for every youngster playing in the wet grass, something Kira thought she would never have. What was her birthright?

She spotted Alex under the canopy with his arm around his grandmother and Lorett by his side. In a flash, she remembered him press against her in the darkness, his grief overwhelming and unbearable.

The body of John "Big Bear" Harper was lowered into the ground and the chanting and drums continued as the crowd dispersed. Richard walked toward her, smiling. He thanked her for coming, gripping her outstretched hand firmly with both of his. "You didn't have to stand so far away. Feel welcome here."

She couldn't express how sorry she felt and her words seemed empty. He invited her to join them at the community center. "There will be more dancing and singing. Many of the people here haven't been together in a long time. While it's a sad time, it's also a time to celebrate his passing into the Spirit World where he'll join our ancestors." Kira didn't want to impose.

Alex approached holding a huge black umbrella over himself and Lorett, who clung to his arm. His eyes never turned to Kira as he told his father that his grandmother wanted to sit by the grave a while longer. Richard ordered Alex to stay with her and took Lorett to help make sure everything was set up at the center. The pair walked down the hill to the truck to join the line of cars leaving the cemetery. Alex glanced back at his grandmother sitting by her husband's grave. He thanked Kira for coming as he surveyed the field of gravestones.

"I wanted to."

Still looking vacantly passed her, he thanked her for the story she had written on his grandfather's life, much more than he had expected from the newspaper.

"Your grandfather was a significant man in his community. It was the least the newspaper could do."

He looked again at the old woman seated gracefully on a metal fold-up chair, her hands resting on her lap. "Look, I'm sorry, about the other night. I shouldn't have—"

"I'm glad you came to me. If nothing else, we can be friends. Your friendship would mean a lot to me."

His family would never be just another news story — Alex meant more to her than that. She acknowledged that he was more than an exotic excursion from her own life, he was a man filled with a myriad of emotions that equaled or surpassed her own sentiments about the world, a man who survived his struggles to finally find his path, a man she truly respected. She didn't know how to tell him, or whether she should say anything at all. He started to speak, but hesitated and his gaze flickered away. Then he said: "I once asked my grandfather why life was so unfair. He said we choose our horse and ride it as best we can. Only, the horse I want to ride isn't the one that will continue PawPaw's dream. It's not the one my father expects me to choose."

She reached out and squeezed his hand. He pulled her to him and hugged her tightly. The umbrella slipped to the ground and she pressed her face into his shirt knowing his decision would take him farther away from her. She stepped back as he let her go and he returned to his grandmother's side. Turning to leave, Kira heard the woman call her.

"Ah, it's the reporter." Elaine thanked Kira for the extended obituary. "Not too many of our own get that kind of respect," she said.

"I'm so sorry." Kira wanted to say more but fell silent.

"I loved my husband with such a force that not even his death can destroy it. And his love for me remains forever strong in my heart." Elaine nodded firmly. "We'll be together again."

Kira listened to the woman's soft voice and felt comforted by her words — but wasn't she the one who should be comforting the woman who had lost her husband? No grief showed in Elaine's eyes, which were clear and bright. Wisps of hair fell over her face that now suddenly appeared as young as Kira's despite the lines of age. They were no longer wrinkles but pathways littered with stories of love and life. Kira watched Alex escort his grandmother to a nearby car, and whispered goodbye to them both.

30

THE PICTURE of Margaret James covered most of the top half of the newspaper's Metro section. Margaret James, Fort Lewis's first female city manager. The story Kira had been planning to do for the Features section. The woman she had been trying to schedule an interview with for almost a month. Kira spread the page out on her desk and checked the byline. Aaron Gant. She narrowed her eyes, staring at the printed name, and almost drew blood as she bit down on her lower lip. Aaron Gant. Why did he not know she was pursuing this story? It had been included in the story assignment list distributed last week. He should have known. And if he didn't know, his editor should have known enough to tell him this story was already being covered.

She chewed on her cheek, breathing rapidly, reading the words that didn't register in her brain because her mind was berating Gant for not coming to her first about writing the story. Gripping the page, she stood up. Her boss happened by, so Kira stopped her to say that Aaron had done her story, but Cicely seemed confused. Kira displayed the page and repeated her explanation. Cicely surveyed the story, said she would take it off the schedule, and headed toward her office. Kira attempted to plead her case again, but Cicely didn't seem to understand why Kira was upset. Typical of Cicely to completely miss the point that Gant should have respected that the Features department already had this story. She wandered into the newsroom, looking for Gant, still pondering how she would approach him. At his desk, he clicked furiously on his keyboard. Tentatively, she stepped closer and said his name.

"What?" He stared at the computer screen.

"The story on Margaret James. I was supposed to do that."

He continued to type. "Oh yeah?"

"Yes. It was on the schedule. Didn't you see it?"

"No."

"Aaron!"

"I'm on deadline."

She moved next to the computer and shook the newspaper in his face to get his full attention. "Don't you read the assignment list?"

He stopped typing and looked at her, offering a thick sigh in response.

"This was my story and I don't appreciate you grabbing it from under me," she said.

"You weren't fast enough. I'm in city hall every day. The opportunity arose, so I took it."

"I wasn't fast enough?" She didn't consider herself a woman prone to violence, but the urge to pummel his face clouded her thoughts. "We don't work for competing newspapers. You could have told me you wanted the story and we could have worked on it together. This is a quick hit, not an in-depth piece on who she is. I had two interviews already done with people she works with that you could have used for background."

"I work alone." He turned his gaze back to his work and began click-clicking once again. Kira envisioned pushing his face into the screen and seeing his dyed blonde hair catch fire. Instead, she threw the newspaper at him and said: "Pity you spelled 'manager' wrong. I wonder what Margaret James will think when she sees she's the city *manger*."

Glancing back at him as she walked away, Kira saw him checking the story.

ENOUGH WAS enough. She threw clothes and toiletries in her overnight bag and dialed Kenny's number. His machine answered and at the beep, Kira told her brother she was on her way to visit and that he better be there to greet her. Frustrated with the lack of respect she was receiving at *The Fort Lewis Times*, she had followed up on her resume at the *Washington Post* and had gotten a call for an interview. The timing could not have been better. This could be her chance to get away, to leave everything behind, a chance to start fresh.

Her spirits began to lift as she drove through the mountains with the summer sun on her face. She stuck a tape in the cassette player and instantly Keith Washington crooned about a lost love. Quickly ejecting it, she scrambled around for something more upbeat. Kira couldn't handle a four-hour ride listening to love songs. Nothing else within reach, she opted instead for the rushing wind around the vehicle and the sound of her own voice singing out of tune to the radio.

Washington, D.C., would be a cool place to live for a year or so and would give her solid experience to move on to New York, maybe. Her mother would like that she was near Kenny for his last year in grad school. And it wasn't so far away that she couldn't visit her mother on a regular basis. Following her scribbled directions and vague memory from her last visit a year before, she found his street, pulled into a parking space, grabbed her bag and bounded into his apartment building. Kira banged on his door and yelled, "Police! Open up." In seconds the door burst open. Kenny leaped out, grabbed Kira around the waist and swung her in a circle. He howled as he pushed her inside and drenched her in congratulations on her interview. As she filled him in on the latest news about his hometown, Kira was interrupted by a man's voice. A face peeked out from one of the back bedrooms. A young man, about her brother's age, appeared in the hallway. He wore a tank top and sweatpants and his skin was the color of a sweet gum leaf in autumn. She looked to her brother for an introduction. Kenny grinned and shook his head at his sister.

"This is my roommate, Tenor."

"Well, how you doing, Tenor?" she said.

He apologized for interrupting and gave Kenny a message to

pass along to his mother if she called. He hoisted his backpack over his shoulder and headed to class. Kira watched his tight butt as he walked out.

"Before you ask," Kenny said, "he's a music major from North Carolina and yes, he's available, but no, you are not gonna get involved with him. He's too young for you."

"How old?"

"Just turned 21."

"Hey, that's legal."

"He's a nice guy," Kenny said. "Not your type at all."

Kira mocked a frown.

DURING A tour of the newsroom, she imagined herself part of the team, a much more multicultural team than at home, she noted. She sat in on a reporter's meeting and talked with several editors including the managing editor who probed her about her career with the *Charlotte Observer* and *The Fort Lewis Times*. She felt good when she left, but not entirely confident that she had gotten the job. She decided not to fret over it, although as she sat on the Metro, watching professional men and women of all colors and sizes quick-walking this way and that at each stop, the idea of living and working in D.C. thrilled her. The city held a vibrant energy that was exhilarating. But did she have the nerve to move to a city where the journalism was cutthroat? Did she have what it would take to find and write compelling stories big-city readers would want? She was a small-town girl, with small-town experience … and maybe with small-town ambition. She wanted the chance to prove herself, to work with journalists who could help her grow and become a better reporter. She wanted a chance to make her life mean something, to make a connection that lasted longer than one night.

Kenny was playing video games on the computer when she got back and immediately quizzed her on her afternoon, but she gave him the impression she was unconcerned and convinced him it wasn't a big deal if she got the job or not. What she really wanted to share with him was about Larry Walsh. Beyond being surprised, she wasn't sure how Kenny would react, but as her brother, she had to tell him.

The words came awkwardly as she told him about their mother's announcement. She told him about the Midnight Club, the band, the trumpet, the coffee with him, the truck driving and the friend on Brighton Place. And then she told him he was white. Kenny swiveled in the chair and stared blankly at his sister, leaving the monster suspended in action in cyberspace.

"What did you say? He's white? Ma was with a white man? Get outta here!" He got up and went to the kitchenette. Kira followed him and tugged at her thumbnail with her teeth. Kenny took a can of Dr Pepper from the refrigerator, snapped it open and stared, mouth open, like a cartoon drawing on a page. His forehead wrinkled and his expression shifted from shock to confusion. "Ma was with a white truck driver? Ain't that some shit. Why'd she say he was dead?"

Kira shrugged and, like a little girl, tagged behind Kenny as he went back into the sitting room and flopped on the couch. Kira leaned against the computer desk. She told him about Larry Walsh visiting their mother at her house. Kenny sat staring at the floor, his head rhythmically shaking "no way" like a bobble head.

"I don't know what I'm supposed to do," she said. Kira struggled to imagine Larry Walsh visiting during the holidays, exchanging gifts, sitting down to dinner together, remembering her birthday. She couldn't picture calling him, seeking advice about her career or a boyfriend. The thought almost made her laugh out loud.

"You know he ain't shit, Kira," Kenny said. "Don't go thinking he's gonna be your daddy now, cause he ain't. It don't take courage to visit your children." Her brother closed his eyes, his head still shaking from side to side. "It don't mean nothing."

Kira squirmed. Kenny always had a way of making her feel like the younger sibling. Not out of spite. As far as her brother was concerned, Kenny was the man of the family. And as he had stretched past Kira in height he had come to feel more protective of her.

"You're always so desperate, Kira. You cling to anything that comes along." He sat resting the soda can on his lap looking down his nose at her with half closed eyes. "Don't forget you're a queen, Sister, and you don't need to settle for nothin." Then he rose suddenly from his seat and went to the bathroom.

Kira yelled after him, "Just because you're studying philosophy doesn't mean you know everything!"

Kira sat cross-legged on the floor. She had never considered herself desperate and the thought made her uncomfortable. Is that how people saw her? She thought about the various men she had been with over the years, many whose names she couldn't remember now. She thought back to high school, to Paul, to how she had given herself to him for fear he would leave her otherwise. Had she been desperate then? What was she possibly desperate for now?

When her brother returned she told him Larry Walsh had AIDS.

"I was thinking about going to see him, but since he didn't tell me himself, I'm not sure. I'm thinking that maybe he wanted to tell me, but maybe he was afraid. I wasn't exactly nice to him."

"So now that he's dying, he wants to see his child."

"Kenny, don't be like that. What would you do if your father was dying?"

"Shoot, he may as well already be dead."

THEY WENT shopping and Kira bought him some music by a rapper she had never heard of before, and a pair of Nike basketball sneakers. They weren't the expensive ones he wanted, the ones Kira wished she could have bought, but he liked them all the same. The next morning, she kissed her brother's sleepy face before heading out the door.

When she got home, Kira called her boss and explained she had a family emergency and would be gone for the rest of the week. She rarely took a vacation and every year lost at least a week that hadn't been used, so she had plenty of days to take off. She booked an afternoon flight to Tennessee and packed. She put her camera in her overnight bag, then took it out. She didn't quite envision them posing for pictures. Then again, maybe they would. She put it back in.

Kira arrived in Knoxville before four o'clock and got a taxi to the scribbled address Clara had given her. The driver dropped her off outside a brick tenement building. Number Sixteen-Eleven was in the basement. A sour stench stung her nose as she descended the concrete steps. She tapped her knuckles on the brown door, waited several moments then knocked again. The door squeaked open. A man with salt-and-pepper hair that may not have been combed in several days looked at her over a chain.

"Wha' you want?"

"Is Larry here?"

"No he ain't."

"Do you know when he'll be back?"

"Who you?"

Unsure of how much this man knew, she said, "A friend. I've come a long way and I need to see him."

"You kin to Carla?"

"You know Carla? She was the one told me I could find Larry here."

"I met her once." The man scratched his unshaven chin. "Ain't sure when he'll be back, but I guess you can come in and wait for him if you like."

She hesitated. "Maybe there's a coffee house nearby?"

"I dunno about nothing like that, but I ain't gonna hurt you. You'll be safer in here. You don't wanna be hanging around on these streets unless you're a cop."

She stepped into a darkened living room. An old couch sat along the back wall with a coffee table covered with magazines.

"I work nights," he said.

"I'm sorry. I had no idea."

"Of course you didn't."

"Are you Roscoe?"

The man nodded. He was short and wore an old faded t-shirt and baggy sweat pants over a thick frame. Early fifties, Kira guessed. He invited her to make herself at home — there were drinks in the refrigerator and leftover chicken if she was hungry — then he strode down a narrow hallway toward the back of the apartment to get more sleep. She pulled open the curtain on the high window allowing light to filter into the compact sitting room. She couldn't see how to open the window, and wished she could let in fresh air to clear away the stink of cigarettes that seemed to coat her skin. A dining table with three chairs was outside the narrow kitchen. The refrigerator held nothing more than four cans of Busch beer, a box of fried chicken and cheese molding in its plastic wrapper. Kira considered the beer then opted for a glass of water. She rinsed out a plastic cup from the cupboard, filled it from the faucet and took a seat on the shabby couch. She waited. She thought about what to say, that she appreciated him for letting her know he cared, that she had always wanted him in her life, that despite everything she wasn't angry, that she wanted to be the daughter he perhaps had hoped for, that he didn't have to be the perfect father. But it all sounded trite. She flipped through a magazine she had picked up at the airport and thought about her book sitting on the kitchen table, forgotten on her way out the door. She waited.

Three hours and twenty-five minutes passed before a key rattled the lock. Larry Walsh shuffled into the apartment carrying a paper bag. Kira stood to attention, her heart battering her chest, as he closed the door behind him. He turned and grunted from fright, dropping the bag and spilling cans of food on the floor.

"What in Jesus' name—?"

Kira immediately kneeled to collect the cans and Larry crouched next to her.

"I'm sorry," she began, but her tongue glued itself to the roof of her mouth. They grabbed at the cans refilling the bag then stood a foot away from each other. "I didn't mean . . ." Kira said. "I wanted to surprise you, but I didn't mean to—"

Larry groaned through a scowl and took the bag into the kitchen. She followed him and watched him restock the empty shelves. She started to chatter uncontrollably, trying to apologize, trying to explain herself. He turned and looked at her for a long time as if he wasn't sure how to respond. He chewed his lower lip, but said nothing.

"I know about . . . you having . . ." She didn't want to say AIDS. It didn't feel right that she should be talking to him about something so personal, so devastating. "I know, and it's okay."

He continued to stare at her. "It ain't okay."

"No, I don't mean—"

"Shit." He turned away from her and leaned on the countertop. "You were right. I never shoulda looked for you. I just wanted to see if maybe I'd created something good in this world."

"I know I didn't give you a very good impression before, but I'm really not a bad person."

He faced her again, a deep frown denting his forehead. "So you find out I'm dying and now you care?"

At first she said nothing. What could she say to that? Then, "It woke me up. Made me realize I'd made a mistake."

His head tilted as he looked at her and the frown faded. "It took me a helluva lot longer to realize that for myself." He turned away, facing the sink. "I'm glad you changed your mind about me."

When her stomach gave a loud rumble, she offered to make something for them to eat and he gladly accepted — he hated cooking. Larry suggested spaghetti and meat sauce, pulled out a jar and a packet of pasta, and helped her find the pots. There were no wooden spoons, just one large plastic serving spoon that she stirred the sauce with. When she asked for a colander, Larry gave her a puzzled expression.

"Never mind," she chuckled.

The apartment soon filled with the tangy smell of the sauce and while the food simmered, she quizzed him.

"There ain't that much to tell." He took a can of Busch from the fridge, took a sip and settled at the dining table. After his military service, he worked in an auto repair shop for a while in Knoxville. Then he went out to California for a time doing some odd jobs. He met a trucker who convinced him trucking was a lucrative way to make a living. So he invested in a rig, got his license.

"I've been driving all over the damn place since." He smiled. He was good-looking in a plain sort of way, and Kira imagined her mother falling for his boyish grin and that dimple in his cheek. He had been married once. Lasted five years and then he had walked out in favor of a struggling actress in Los Angeles. That didn't last either. He wasn't impressed with marriage and preferred to hook up with someone not interested in owning him.

"Most of my friends are either divorced or dead now. And my folks, well they're grumpy and old, living separate lives in the same house in Nashville. I don't never wanna be like that."

"Do they know about me?"

He waited a moment before slowly shaking his head. "They ain't racists, but they think folks should keep to their own, if you know what I mean. And I didn't turn out to be what they had hoped. We don't talk much."

"My aunt said your father taught piano classes."

Larry's face widened with a broad smile. "You're aunt Mae was something. A beauty, just like your mother. Didn't Mae take lessons from my dad? No, it was her friend. Mae was a good-looking lady, but too old for me. When I met your mother, I knew they was family."

His father had taught high-school music until he retired a few years ago. He had taught Larry to play the piano and the trumpet.

"I used to love to play the trumpet. Jazz. The Blues." He shook his head. "I lost the love for it though after the war. I played Taps so many times I lost count. Life just kinda fell away from me after that. Shit, I'm talking too much. Tell me about you."

She shared with him her decision to become a journalist, her job at *The Fort Lewis Times*, that she had a brother at American University and that she was hoping to move to a bigger city.

"You ain't married yet?"

Kira laughed. "No, not yet. Maybe one day. No strong candidates so far. Tell me about meeting my mother."

"Such a long time ago and yet like yesterday. She could dance and seemed to laugh about all the time. Full of fun. Didn't have no cares. Neither of us did. Just having a good time."

Kira pictured her mother, a young woman, dancing and laughing with Larry Walsh, thinking about nothing more than having a good time. "Did you love her?"

He shook what little beer there was left in the can. "I ain't gonna lie and say it was love. I don't think she was in love with me neither. But I cared about her a lot. She was a good woman. Still is."

Kira asked him about Carla and he described her as a friend he had known for years.

"When I show up, she always gives me all she has. Feeds me, listens to me and gives me a place to sleep. Never demands nothing of me."

He went into the kitchen and retrieved several bottles of pills from the counter. He returned to the table with a glass of water and methodically opened each container. With each pill he took a gulp. "I'm supposed to take these at the same time every day," he said. "I get tired of taking them, but I got to."

Kira asked him when he discovered he had contracted the virus. He wasn't sure how he had gotten it — could have been from a prostitute or a dirty needle. Kira tried not to show her shock, and nodded as she would if interviewing someone for a news story.

"I ain't never been no angel, but I've been living with this for the past ten years trying to do right. It started out as HIV. You can live with that for a long time, but the last few years it changed. The doctor says it's AIDS now, which means my day's coming soon. Now, I guess, I'm trying to make my life mean something."

"It means something to me."

He paused, his dimple creasing his cheek. "I'm running outta money. Got nothing to give you. Didn't give you nothing all your life. And I'm sorry about that. I truly am."

Kira nodded. "You helped give me life."

He shrugged. "Well, don't waste it. I did a whole lotta fooling around and taking life for granted. I blamed your mama for not wanting me around, but I never made the effort to be there for you. It was easy to blame someone else. And all these years, I missed out on something that was real important." He fell silent and finished the water.

Their lives were worlds apart, but it didn't matter. They had made a connection, and even if it were only for this day, Kira had a father she would respect and remember, not with bitterness, but with fondness; despite their differences and the silent years between them, he had cared and had finally made the effort to let her know it.

They said good-bye in the early morning. He reached out to shake her hand, but she felt compelled to hug him. Although his arms remained at his sides, she felt the embrace was more fitting. It surprised her how frail he felt in her arms. He promised to visit her again soon, and she promised to write.

She would never see him again. He would die a year later. But she had a photograph that Larry's roommate had taken while they sat at the dining table, and a note Larry had written around Christmas time saying he had never felt better.

31

THE MORNING sun streaked across the stairs illuminating dust particles suspended in the air. Still sleepy, Alex took one step at a time down from his apartment to the shop. He could hear his father whistling. It wasn't unusual but it seemed chirpier, sharper perhaps. Alex wasn't sure, but it sounded different. He smelled breakfast.

"Coffee and biscuits are in the back," Richard said, without looking around as Alex pushed through the beaded curtain. His mouth full of food, Alex gave a muffled response that he had found the sausage biscuits. His father balanced himself on a stool near the entrance. He had hung the wooden plate Alex had given him for his birthday and beneath it he was adding a sign. Alex kept quiet and watched until his father moved so he could read what the sign said. He washed the dry biscuit down with coffee and waited. Richard needlessly dusted the plate, then stepped down from the stool and stood back to check his work.

Not for Sale. Three Generations of Harpers by Alex Harper.

Alex read the sign over and over, each time looking at the plate to make sure it was the same one he had painstakingly carved, mostly at night, over a period of weeks. The same one his father had barely acknowledged. Richard turned and beamed at Alex, who looked at his father, then looked again at the sign his father had neatly hand-written on white poster board with a black marker: *Not for Sale. Three Generations of Harpers by Alex Harper.*

"It's the best thing you've ever done," Richard said. "Seemed to me there was no better place than to have it where everyone could see it. Don't you think so?"

Alex stared from his father to the plate, and back to his father.

"Well, let's get to work," Richard said, picking up the stool and heading to the back office. "We can't be standing around here all day looking at each other."

Alex grabbed his grandfather's stool and set it outside the door to honor his memory. He saw MawMaw ambling down the hill toward the store in the same manner his PawPaw had done so many times before. He waited for her to arrive.

"What you doing out here?" Elaine asked, holding a basket of sandwiches on her arm. "I know your Paw's expecting you to be inside working on those books."

Alex surveyed the clear sky. "I'm just checking to see if pigs are flying today."

"What are you talking about, boy?"

"Paw hung the plate I gave him for his birthday in the store for everyone to see."

"Didn't your PawPaw say he was proud of it."

"Yes, he did."

NERVOUS, ALEX sat next to his father at the lead table in the community center, and on the other side of Richard sat MawMaw. His father was presiding over the first meeting of the Committee of Clans since PawPaw's death. Richard had stepped into PawPaw's role — the committee members' votes had been unanimous. They would vote again to bring Alex onto the committee to fill his father's role. No opposition had surfaced and the Harper family would continue to lead the community as it had done for decades. He had almost skipped the meeting altogether, deciding instead to walk through the woods — if he weren't present, the committee would surely vote him down. But he heard his PawPaw's words, *You're our future, Alex*, and at the last minute he ran to the center and arrived just as his father was about to open the meeting.

Richard announced that the Cherokee Nation in Oklahoma

had contributed significant monies that, with the matching grant from the Floyd Nature Preserve, would allow them to make a bid on Mrs. Foster's land for sure and put them close enough for more negotiation with Harry Newcomb. The room filled with cheers and applause.

Alex leaned forward and stole a peek at MawMaw — she glowed. He surveyed the committee members, wise men and women, most significantly older than he, each representing their own clan. Strange that he now sat among them, poised to help guide the Cherokees of the Virginias into the next century. He felt daunted by the responsibility, yet thinking about his grandfather, he wanted to make a difference. There was ample opportunity to represent his generation and move the community forward. First, he would take advantage of new technologies: computers that could tell the world about who they were, about their goal to continue purchasing land, about expanding the community center and growing the museum there. He could convert the apartment above Big Bear's Cabin into a studio for his work and use the store to feature new up-and-coming Indian artists. An excitement at the possibilities swelled inside him.

When the meeting ended, he shook one hand after another as people acknowledged him as a bonafide member of the committee.

Lorett hovered, waiting for a moment to get close and hug him tightly. Alex halfheartedly returned the embrace. His father stood at the door, waving to folks heading home for the night. He asked his son to lock up; he was heading home and straight to bed. For a moment, he pondered Alex and Lorett before giving them a thin smile. Alex saw his grandfather in his father's eyes. Suddenly, he felt the urge to rush to his father and hold him close. Alex couldn't remember when he had last told his father he loved him. As Richard turned to leave Alex called him back. He said the words, "I love you," letting them flow easily through his lips. His father stared at him for a moment before nodding as if he had always known. Quietly, he slipped out of the building.

"Your father is the sweetest man I know, next to you," Lorett said. "He's coping well. And your grandmother, too. She's a strong woman."

Alex stepped away from Lorett and stared down at the dusty wooden floor. "It needs to be stained," he said, absently.

"Huh?"

He turned to her. She ran her fingers over her scar and looked at him through hair that had fallen over her eyes. A light beamed through her dress and he saw the curves of her body. He had made love to that body more times and in more places than he could remember. Yet, he had been unfaithful more than he wanted to admit. He still cared for her, although not as he once had when they were innocent teenagers learning about love and exploring sex. For all he knew, he had been her first and only, and guilt sometimes beleaguered him. But her smothering love, her blind devotion choked him. For a while, pursuing other women gave him air to breathe. With PawPaw gone, time had changed. Alex was forced to change, too, and accept his role as a future leader of the clan. His father expected him to continue the Harper line and, after the funeral, he had made another effort with Lorett. Nonetheless, being a husband to Lorett wouldn't make either of them happy. His decision had been made and he stumbled over words he knew would cut deeply. He could not marry her. She screamed and pounded her fists on his chest, forcing him backwards; she begged him to change his mind and, for the briefest moment, he almost relented. Hadn't she waited for him while he went off to explore his art and to find himself? Weren't both her family and his waiting for this moment? He had never meant to hurt her, but without a doubt, marriage would create the greatest pain for them both. He let her curse him, punch him until she almost doubled over, exhausted. Drained of all force, she left him standing in the center, alone.

There were two Harper men left. He felt like part of the nursery rhyme. Three little Indians. Two little Indians. Only two left. All eyes on him to lead and continue the line into the future. He didn't know about the future; he couldn't think beyond this moment. He wished Andy were still here; he would have sheltered Alex from all responsibility. With a deep sigh, he locked the door and stuffed the key into his pocket. He would take it one step at a time.

~

KIRA SIPPED her coffee and spread the newspaper out on the kitchen table. Before she could spread her toast with jam, the picture caught her attention. A black man wearing orange prison coveralls scowled from the front page of the metro section. Slouching in his seat with his lips pursed as if there should have been a toothpick between them. His name was Donnell Johnson, and he had been convicted of breaking and entering, grand larceny and possession of a firearm last year and was now serving ten years in the state prison. He claimed he had been strung out on crack at the time of the robbery. The story was the second in Aaron Gant's occasional series on crime. It went on to recount the increase in crimes around the city and held up Johnson as an example of what the city was doing about the problem. Kira noted that all the quotes were from residents who lived in the more affluent white neighborhoods, who talked about having installed security systems in their homes. Kira shook her head. He had done it again.

She stormed into the newsroom and immediately sought him out.

"What the hell is this?" she asked, throwing the Metro section on Aaron's desk. He didn't look up but he held a faint smile.

"Do your friends give you a new swastika with every story you write against black folks?" she asked.

Aaron looked up at her then, his grin gone, but still he said nothing.

"When are you going to investigate the rampant drug use among white residents? Or maybe you're trying to divert the attention away from your relatives?"

"I don't have to put up with this. The series is done."

"But it's an *occasional* series," she said. "Who would know if you were to add another story to it? You think you're up to it? Think you can open your mind a little?"

He ignored her and began typing rapidly on the keyboard.

"Can't you take one sympathetic look at the black community just once to see things from a different perspective?"

He snorted. "It's not my fault the crime comes out of y'all people's neighborhoods."

Kira shook her head. "You know, people told me you were an asshole, and I thought maybe they were stretching the truth," she said. "You know how people do. But I believe, in this case, they were being nice."

She smiled and casually turned, heading for Barker's office. Barker held the phone to his ear but beckoned her in. She stood clutching the paper in her hand, fending off her shuddering nerves. He finally hung up and asked what she needed. She inhaled. "When are we going to do a series on white crime?"

He frowned. "What do you mean?"

Kira pointed to the picture illustrating Aaron's series, then flicked through the pages to a two-paragraph story opposite the obituary page on a man who had been arrested for sexually assaulting a ten-year-old girl. His race was not mentioned.

"Statistics show pedophiles are white men," she said. "When are we going to do an expose on them? We constantly publish these miniscule stories in the back pages on whites who have committed crimes, yet we parade on the front page stories of black men in jail. Don't you think we should be presenting a more balanced picture of our community?"

Barker rapidly tapped a pencil on his desk and watched her silently. She stared back at him, waiting for a response. All she could hear was his tap-tapping in time with her heart beat. He looked at his desk then snapped his fingers.

"Why don't you and Gant work on a story together?"

Kira took a moment to digest what he had said. She hadn't been looking for an assignment, simply some balanced crime reporting.

"This is obviously important to you," Barker said. "I'll talk to Gant, and I'll tell features you'll be on a special assignment for the next few weeks. How about that? Finish up whatever you're currently working on, then you and Gant can get started."

Kira wasn't sure what to say and stared at him wondering if he was serious. She wondered if he knew she had been planning to leave the paper and move on to better things. Just this week, she had received a couple of thanks-but-no-thanks letters from some newspapers she had applied to but was hopeful the *Washington Post* would call. She thought about Alex's decision to stay and support his people. She thought about Beverly asking if running away was the answer. Blacks never stayed long at the paper to get invested enough to fight for change, she had said. After five years at the newspaper, Kira had to get invested and make change.

Barker slid his glasses up his nose and asked her if that was okay. She nodded, then stood dumbfounded outside his office before meandering back to her desk. Almost bursting with the news, she searched the newsroom for Beverly. When she spied Aaron talking to one of the editors, she began to laugh. He would hate working with her and would probably fight her every step of the way, but she had worked the crime beat before and knew her way around a courthouse. This was a challenge she would enjoy. Suddenly exhilarated, she shouted across the room, "Aaron! Looks like we'll be working together."

He gaped at her, obviously puzzled, and she beamed.

ALEX SAT on her front step, but she resolved not to let him in, not to continue whatever strange relationship they had started. With him engaged to marry someone else, she would only get hurt. She had said they could be friends, but now she wasn't sure. Kira had resolved to start afresh — no more games, no more relationships based on sex, no more men telling her what she should be. After grabbing her grocery bags from the car, she approached him with a smile, ready to turn him away. He stood up, wearing jeans, a black t-shirt, hair tied neatly behind his head and an expression that was clearly happy to see her. She faltered and then regrouped.

"Alex, it's good to see you, but … but we can't keep doing this. I can't—"

"I brought you this." He held out a small paper sack.

Reluctantly, she invited him inside where she could dump her groceries in the kitchen and politely receive his gift. They stood together in the sitting room as she opened the bag. Inside was a velvet pouch and from that she pulled the wolf pendant. Immediately, she protested, but he insisted.

"It reminds me of you," he said.

What could she say? "We can't keep seeing each other."

"I'm not marrying Lorett. I don't love her anymore." He stared at her earnestly.

The words slowly seeped in until she realized what he was saying. "Since when?" she blurted. "Why all of a sudden this change of heart?" Still clutching the pendant, she sat on the edge of the couch.

"It hasn't been all that sudden. I've known for a long time, I just didn't have the guts to admit it. We were kids when we fell in love, and I grew out of it a long time ago, even before New Mexico." He sat next to her. "The trouble was, I had promised her, and she had waited for me. I felt obligated to marry her. But that's no way to begin a future with someone."

He kept talking, explaining that he had stepped into the leadership role for his community, but he wouldn't sacrifice everything. He wanted to *share* his life, not surrender it to someone else's ideals.

"I've been wandering aimlessly through this life, Kira, running from labels and expectations, letting other people define me. Since coming back home, I've had a chance to stand still long enough to see an open landscape ahead of me, one that I can carve into any shape and paint any color. I can create my own life and still make it meaningful to my people and to myself." He paused as if to ponder his words. "I'm not sure whether or not who I am fits into your world, but I'd like to include you in mine."

Kira looked at the wolf pendant, rubbing her thumb over its surface. She noticed Alex's hand, poised to grab hers and pull her off the sidelines. He had once gotten her to jump and spin wildly, to lose her self-consciousness, and be free. The memory made her smile. She could enjoy what they had in common and learn much from what was different, but more than anything, she wanted simply to continue the dance.

32

*I*VE RAISED *my family as I was raised. Taught them what I was taught. It's what I know. Our people have been fractured, our language lost to many, our true way of life essentially destroyed. We're not now what we once were, but the future won't stop for us to catch up. We have to do the best we can to move forward, to regain some of what's lost and continue the traditions we still have. My family is the link between then and now. My grandson, Alex, is the link to what's ahead for us. I have told our story so my son and his son, and his son, can continue telling the story, adding new chapters with each new generation. This story is who we were, who we are now, and what we can become. If we can secure this land, our story will blossom. We can firmly establish our unity. It will not die with me, but will live on through the future Cherokees of the Virginias. You're one of the world's record keepers. So I share with you the life of my people and you can share it with the rest of the world.*

CPSIA information can be obtained at www.ICGtesting.com
Printed in the USA
LVOW120314110112

263323LV00001B/76/P